Manitoba Tea & Tarot Mysteries

MOONSHINE, MAGIC & MURDER

JANUARY BAIN

Moonshine, Magic & Murder
ISBN # 978-1-83943-977-3
©Copyright January Bain 2021
Cover Art by Erin Dameron-Hill ©Copyright May 2021
Interior text design by Claire Siemaszkiewicz
Totally Bound Publishing

MOONSHINE, MAGIC & MURDER

Dedication

Dedicated to the positive energy of the universe,
where all things are possible.
And to the beautiful people who serve it.
A special thanks to my brilliant editor, Rebecca,
who knows more about crafting a story than
anyone I know.
Heartfelt thanks to the wonderful people at
Totally Bound Publishing for making the journey
so wonderful.
And to the wonderful man who shares his life so
fully with me, a thank you would never be
enough. I'm humbled and honored to be with
you.
And to the real baby Ling Ling, thanks for the
inspiration!

Chapter One

The universe looks less like a big machine than a big thought.
Dean Radin, PhD

"Careful! That box is already spelled! Anything could happen if you mix them up," I shouted at my triplet Star, who was paying me no mind, just moving things haphazardly around as she 'dusted' the shelves of the Tea & Tarot café.

Star twitched her whole body into a pretend robot, her blonde curls bouncing when she dime-stopped her limbs in an abrupt series of motions. It was a lightning change of mood that had become far too common of late. I gave a deep sigh of frustration I didn't bother to hide. She'd been getting worse by the day, antsy no doubt for The Call. *Darn movie people. Telling her she had a role, then delaying production.*

"Oh, *really.*" Okay, she was good at the robot dance, I'd give her that, if a job ever asked for such a dubious ability. But that didn't stop me from rushing forward to rescue the Promise Bags. They held the precious trinkets of all the females around town who were participating in the upcoming Sadie Hawkins dance. Each midnight blue velvet bag had been magically infused with a specific wish, ranging from a marriage proposal to a spa vacation. *Mix up those babies and all Hades will break loose*, because this year the items had been blessed under the decade's most awesome supermoon.

Maybe that's a bad idea? I chewed on a fingernail while I worried about going too far in my overwhelming urge to have my fellow goddesses receive their fair due from men who did not always appreciate them. Men could be so lame sometimes, not reading the signals right under their very noses, though that did not appear to be the case with our local Mountie, Ace Collins. He could be a little too astute at times. *Goddess, give me the strength...*

The emotive notes of a musical instrument native to Scotland, one that defied the noise ordinance of Snowy Lake, broke through my worry fog.

Auntie T.J.

I set the rescued box safely aside on a shelf and scurried toward the huge picture window of the Tea & Tarot café to where Tulip sat perched on a stool. The third triplet of our McCall clan, she was a matching bookend to Star, which made them both polar opposites to me with my Elizabeth Taylor-esque violet-colored eyes and dark hair. Or at least according to Granny Toogood, who loved her old movies.

Tulip was keyboarding as per usual on her computer, working either on her blog posts or selling our newly rolled out 'potcakes' to the Canadian masses. I sent a silent prayer to the goddess that the extra revenue the items were supposed to bring in happened. We'd invested in producing cannabutter to add to our spectacular line-up of bakery goods, and to think it might go to waste if the idea didn't catch on induced serious heart palpitations. *And that just isn't right when a gal's only twenty-one years old.*

"Shoot! What's Auntie T.J. up to now?"

"She only brings out the big guns when she feels threatened," Tulip said. "See, Sergei McCausland." She pointed at the business owner our auntie was serenading with her warmongering.

The town hound dog owned the Bowl-a-ram-a, the five-pin bowling alley tucked away at the outskirts of town, which was located a hop, skip and a jump from our café, Snowy Lake being so small with only twelve hundred and fifty-nine residents, that I could run across it quicker than I could be bothered to start up my Jeep, Thor.

Though that had been changing somewhat of late with the arrival of Constable Collins and his annoying active pursuit of law and order. Sheriff Winn Duffy was more beloved of course, having turned a blind eye for decades, but the new Mountie was gaining ground. *Did I share that he's a handsome devil?*

"What's Hound Dog up to now?" Star asked, joining us behind the counter.

"Star, don't be saying that out loud. Granny Toogood might overhear," I chastised my sister automatically. The woman who had taken us in at eight years old had a thing about swearing and speaking ill of others, among a host of other things that she expected everyone to have learned in kindergarten. I gave a quick glance around the café, taking a second to admire the décor of midnight blue walls with enough glitter to choke a horse, thanks to Star, our resident glitter mistress. *No Granny and no customers at the moment.* Of course, it was an off-time, Sunday morning before church let out.

"Why is she upset with him?" Tulip asked, computer forgotten as she got to her feet to join us. The three of us stood shoulder-to-shoulder and stared at Auntie T.J. in her full Highland dress that was a touch too plaid-mad for my tastes. Her newly tinted burgundy hair with a wide pink streak down one side shone sparkly in the sun and drew attention to the bright slash of siren-red adorning her lips. She stood on the solid-yellow divided line of Main Street and blasted away in the face of the far larger Sergei, who appeared, from his wide-legged stance and wild hand gestures, to be pretty darn angry.

"I heard that he's been manufacturing Auntie's special elixir out at Skull Cave. Pretty much stole her recipe," Star said, punctuating her remarks with a significant raising of her perfectly groomed eyebrows.

"No! Not Auntie T.J.'s Magic Elixir, her special apple pie moonshine?" Tulip asked, her mouth pursing into a rosebud, her eyes as wide as a snowy owl's.

"The cure for whatever ails you." I repeated the oft-heard company slogan. My auntie had a lot of entrepreneurial spirit, I'd give her that, though that might explain our own venture into marijuana edibles, since the Canadian laws had changed a few days ago. *Can't escape DNA.* I pushed past Star to storm out through the front door into the unseasonably warm mid-October morning. The angel chimes overhead went wild with a chorus of *Halleluiah* as I let the door slam shut behind me.

"*Auntie T.J.!*" I screamed at the top of my lungs, wind-milling my arms to get her attention over the caterwauling of the pipes. She either didn't see me or was studiously ignoring me. The sound was even louder this close, and I cringed from the instant eardrum pain, clasping both hands over the sides of my head.

Sergei came right up to me, catching me before I could confront my auntie, grab hold of the 'musical' instrument and tear her fingers from the chanter. Actually, I loved the sound of the bagpipes…when they were located over the hill and moaning into the distance, as they were meant to be enjoyed.

"Would you talk some darn sense into that woman? She's going to drive away all my business. I have half a mind to sue her. Did you know she was at my place this morning before following me here? Nearly drove a van-load of senior citizens away. I had to offer the first game half-price. I can't have that." He shook his head with vigor. "You need to talk to her, make her see sense. Daft old bird."

"What's got her riled? You know she only does this when she's driving away bears or someone's done her wrong," I shouted back.

His expression shifted and his eyes narrowed. "I have no idea. The woman is certifiable. I'm calling the cops if she persists. We'll see what Sheriff Winn Duffy thinks about all this. He'll toss her in jail for disturbing the peace. Mark my words."

I placed my hands on my hips and cocked my head at him. "That's not what I heard. I think you know very well what's going on here."

He flushed darker and didn't look me in the eyes.

"That's what I thought. You stole her Apple Pie Moonshine recipe!" I pointed my forefinger at his broad chest. Sergei stood a full head taller than I am, with me being by far the shortest of the McCall triplets. But nature made up for that by having me born a whole day earlier than my sisters, or one minute to midnight, if I was being specific.

"I didn't steal her darn recipe. I just worked it out for myself. It's not rocket science, you know. I just came downtown to buy some edibles from the Tea & Tarot and this is the thanks I get." He began to pout like a five-year-old. Of course, Auntie T.J. was no better. Granny Toogood's only sister was not only ten years younger than her, but also six decades behind her in the smarts and maturity departments.

"Let me deal with my aunt. You can leave now. I'll have a talk with her."

"You'd better. Just sayin'. Because I'm not putting up with this much longer, missy!"

The blast of the police sirens firing off must have been droned out by the moaning of the pipes, because suddenly there was Constable Ace Collins standing at my side. We'd even missed the flashing lights atop the Royal Canadian Mounted Police SUV.

But my oh my, he was looking handsome this morning, all six-foot-plus, broad-shouldered, narrow-hipped, Stetson-wearing Mountie that he was. He touched his large fingers to his fine hat and nodded at me before turning a steely-eyed glance on Sergei McCausland. Even the bagpipes had silenced with his arrival. Auntie T.J. stood quiet with her fingers poised over the chanter holes in case she needed to punctuate her point yet again. I shook my head at her in an exaggerated motion, a finger to my lips.

"Are you threatening Miss McCall?" he asked. He must have picked up on the recipe-stealing man's last comment. The Bowl-a-ram-a wasn't the sure-fire business plan that Sergei had dreamed of, I suspected, which was probably why he'd gone into manufacturing moonshine. That tempered my thoughts. Business was hard won in a small town, and it was good that he offered people entertainment during the endless months of a typical long and freezing Canadian winter. But still, using my auntie's recipe sucked. She'd spent years fine-tuning it to what she thought her hero from the TV show *Justified's* Mags Bennett's moonshine tasted like, and she was rightly proud of it. I'd enjoyed it on a few occasions myself...when I didn't have to work the following morning.

"No, of course not. I was just wanting a bit of peace, for heaven's sake. That woman's been doing this for three days running. She's trying to ruin my business. You *have* to do something, Constable, or so help me I will go over your head and speak to Winn Duffy. I know you're too fond of the McCall family by half."

Oooh. That last comment was uncalled for. Ace Collins was a man of complete integrity. A straight shooter. A man of conviction. I backed up a couple of steps in the dead silence while the two men glared at each other, then I backed up a bit farther.

A surge of anger forced its way through me. Who did this guy think he was? Casting aspersions on Ace and my family like that? A streetlamp popped nearby, blowing up and showering sparks in the nearby vicinity, which included the three of us. We all ran for cover, well, except for the Mountie, who gave me a look, shaking his head with a steely look on his handsome mug. He flicked a smoldering spark from his sleeve and strolled over to join me standing on the sidewalk in front of the café. Auntie T.J. and Sergei had vanished like vampires at sunrise.

Behind me, I experienced the emotions of my sisters burning into my back. The town was suddenly silent, like the whole universe was holding its collective breath. *Goddess, do not fail me now. I ask for your protection and understanding.* I sent the prayer into the crisp morning air before turning a benevolent smile toward my favorite Mountie.

"Morning, darlin'. I trust you will be talking to your aunt for me? Sharing my concerns over her breaking the town's sound ordinance, jaywalking and obstructing traffic on Main Street laws?"

I glanced around pointedly, about to say that no one was waiting to drive down the street that I could see, when he reached out to take my hand with his far larger and far warmer one, throwing me off-kilter in a heartbeat. I nodded mutely as a momentous electrical charge coursed through me, making me feel I could provide lighting for the entire town. I groaned, only imaging what Tulip was observing with her new-found gift of reading auras. Now she had ammunition up the yin-yang for blackmail or teasing. Had I just lost the oldest sister advantage?

Trying to tug my hand away from his without appearing too obvious about it didn't work. He held on, then did the unexpected — leaned his head down toward me and captured my lips for a kiss. A modest one for certain, quite quick, but oh so memorable. My insides trembled at the pleasurable sensations that rippled through me.

When he pulled his head away, he gave me a certain look from under the brim of his Stetson, then let go of my hand. "Be sure to talk to your aunt or I will."

"Are *you* threatening me?" Hands back on hips, I glared at him with all the emotions our impossible-to-consummate relationship produced. Until we knew for absolute, unequivocally dead certain that he was my one true love, we couldn't do much at all as it might jeopardize my goddess-given gifts.

My searcher gift—finding lost items—wouldn't be missed near as much as my healing gift, because the whole town counted on *that*. And as Granny Toogood had shared a few weeks back, if I gave myself to someone who wasn't The One, I'd lose it all. And the town wasn't helping us a bit on this one. Instead, it was always interrupting us. If we didn't steal kisses on the run, there'd be none at all.

"No, Miss McCall. But consider yourself fully warned of the consequences for your aunt if you don't fix this thing. I don't want to hear it happens for a fourth day." A twitch that I had observed on the odd occasion began in his cheek. He was feeling the effects of our needing to restraint ourselves to only kisses as much as me. *Good. Fair play.* Though, in truth, it was more a hesitation on Ace's part than mine. I was about ninety-nine-point-nine percent certain he was my one. I just had to persuade *everyone* else that it was the case. That my healing gift would stay intact.

"I'll handle it," I said, tucking my hands behind my back while rolling on the balls of my feet. *Nice to see a man sweat.* Not that I didn't want more than a few chaste kisses from Ace, but in the meantime, it was a fun if somewhat frustrating time. And I was pretty sure I knew how it would all end. Or at least I had my hopes.

Another light standard winked as if it too were going to blow. "Oh, relax already. I got this." I turned and headed back into the café, bracing myself for my sister's comments.

Chapter Two

"Well, well, well," Tulip said, her expression smugger than Ling Ling's, our white and apricot Himalayan furry baby, when presented with a choice bit of properly cooked fresh-water trout newly caught in Snowy Lake.

"No time for this. We've got that Northern Lights Coven emergency meeting in ten minutes."

"What? I didn't know we had one today! What's going on?" Tulip asked, her expression shifting instantly.

"We need to do something about Auntie T.J. or our Mountie is going to do it for us." I pulled out my phone and sent out an immediate SOS to my numerous fellow goddesses.

"Ace wouldn't do anything!" Star protested with a laugh.

"Oh yes he will." I raised my eyebrows for emphasis.

"Duh. The man's frustrated," Tulip said, that annoying smugness back once more. "Do you know what you both looked like just then?"

"I don't want to know. Button it," I said, a clear sabre-rattle warning in my tone.

"You were both firing off red sparks in every which direction. Unbelievable." Tulip shook her head, making her blonde curls dance. "You guys are in for it. If you last out the month without heading for home plate, I'd be seriously surprised."

"I wish I could see auras," Star chimed in. "Levitation is just so lame."

"Never mind mine or Ace's aura, what I want to know is what Sergei's and Auntie T.J.'s looked like?" I demanded.

Tulip frowned. "Auntie's was bright and colorful as usual, but Sergei's was awfully dark. Charcoal gray." She shuddered. "It was really odd. Never saw that color before. Though not as weird as the double-aura I saw on Floyd Millhouse last week when I was talking with Betty over at the Lakeside Motel."

"Double-aura? Sounds like a split-personality," I mused, thinking back to our last case of murder in Snowy Lake just a few short weeks before when the movie people had descended on our town and mayhem had broken out. *Hmm, and also a case of double-murder with the ricin and clubbing by two separate individuals. Very strange indeed.*

"And there's something else —" Tulip began.

Ling Ling meowed loudly and rushed into the café from the back kitchen where, I presumed, since I had seen her on the sidewalk earlier, she'd just entered the café through her cat door. She hopped up beside Tulip's computer and meowed loudly at the screen, her right paw bouncing on the keyboard. It would have been business as usual except for her remarkable size. Her fur was standing out in all directions, making her resemble a huge snowball. *Okay, that isn't good.* It usually heralded some information of unsettling import. At least now we had a system to get at it.

"What is it, baby?" Tulip asked. She sat down and peered at the screen. Star and I huddled behind her. "A?" she asked patiently.

No response.

"B?"

When Tulip spoke the letter "G", Ling Ling tapped the keyboard with a definitive paw.

"Okay, second letter?"

"H?" Got the next decisive tap.

Then "O" was signaled and just as the laborious procedure began again, I got it. "Ghost? Are you signaling 'ghost', Ling Ling?"

A series of affirmative happy taps followed.

"Great! Well done, you," I congratulated myself since no one else spoke up or patted me on the back. I usually won this competition. Maybe I was becoming a real-life Dr. Doolittle? This year so many gifts had shown up for the three of us that I couldn't rule it out.

"Ghost?" Star looked less happy. "What ghost?" She began to glance furtively about, like she expected something to jump right out at her. *Ha! Where's that smug robot dance now?*

"No time for this. The coven will be here in minutes. Star, retrieve the grimoires. I want the best protection spells for Auntie T.J. rolled out yesterday." The thought of Sergei's dark cloud bothered me more than I was going to share. I didn't need my sisters focused on ghosts that I considered to be harmless for the most part rather than where it needed to be—protecting our own.

I ran into the back and grabbed a tray of fresh-baked triple-chocolate eclairs and scurried back to rejoin my sisters. I wanted time to consult all three of the goddess-blessed grimoires.

"Oh-oh," Tulip said and turned to face me, her face gone white under the remnants of her summer tan.

I halted in my tracks, still holding the tray of treats. Tulips pressed her nose up against the glass again, looking skyward. "What is it? What's wrong now?"

"The clouds are really upset." She pointed upward. "Look, a face right there."

"Whose face?" I set the tray down and moved closer. At least she didn't mean an earthly body was outside and about to pounce. Clouds, while a potent omen, didn't attack people *per se*.

"The devil's face."

A shiver crept up my spine, mostly from the dire way she said the creepy words. I glanced over at Star, who had unlocked the cupboard that held our coven's grimoires and was now holding the precious artifacts in her white-gloved hands. They were heavy when placed all together and she set the collection down with a loud thump on a wooden table reserved for customers, after pushing aside the placemats.

"No time for the devil today, Tulip. Okay, let's have a gander." I hurried over to Star. This was my job, being firstborn. The books only responded to my prompting and I relished this auspicious moment more than anyone knew.

"Okay, join hands," I instructed. Star slipped off her gloves and the three of us bowed our heads together. "Star to my right, Tulip to my left, the Goddess at my head, let me find favor and grace before all."

We broke apart and Star perched on the edge of the booth. "We also need to find a spell to stop the Hound Dog from speaking ill of Auntie T.J.," she said.

"You want to find a dead toad and extract its tongue?" I asked, trying to hide my smirk. At her look of horror, I quipped, "Thought not."

"And just try getting Auntie to place it in her shoe," Tulip said with a grimace. We were all aware of the old spells. Sometimes I was tempted, I'll admit. If only there was one that would make me six inches taller and my hips three inches slimmer, I'd try that sucker, even if I had to wear a toad's tongue in my shoe for a month.

"Well, at least I'm trying to think of something outside the box," Star said, adding a pouty look for good measure.

"Okay, I need to concentrate for a minute here," I said.

I reverently touched the first tome. The symbol of a stylized eye representing all the goddesses of ancient Egypt along with the accompanying prowling lioness outlined in pure gold against the darkened ancient leather stirred my blood each and every time I laid eyes on them. The text was written in an ancient language and fancy hieroglyphics on parchment with ink that had faded to a reddish hue. The grimoire pulsated with energy, reaching out to me with an irresistible force. I laid my hands flat on the cover and let the power of those who had come before enter my body in heady waves for a full minute before setting the treatise aside.

"How does it feel?" Tulip asked.

"Good, full of the usual energy. Nothing specific reaching out and telling me to look inside." I lived for the day that would happen, that I would be given a sign across the centuries. *A gal can hope.*

I turned to the second grimoire that was actually two in one, both re-bound together in a leather cover. One was written by Reginald Scot, *Discoverie of Witchcraft,* published in 1584. The majority of the spells, wisdoms, exorcisms, charms, talismans and rituals for conjuring up treasure and enclosing a spirit in crystal the tome contained we knew to be safe. They were tried and true ways to deal with dicey situations when protective measures were called for. The ones we didn't understand as yet, we didn't touch with a ten-foot pole.

The second half was a version of the original *Clavicula Solomonis* or *Key of Knowledge,* titled the *Key of Solomon* from 1572, which gave instructions on how to summon spirits but without the full listing of the demons, which I always ignored, more than certain we'd never be involved with *that* alarming process. Just thinking about it made me shudder. If toad tongues were bad, this grimoire would have blown the lid right off the Crock-Pot. It seemed to me the vilest things were reserved for turning invisible. *Must be one hard-earned process.* Well, they did use still-beating hearts in their game plan.

But the best part of this more practical grimoire, at least the first section, was that the spidery writing of my eighth-removed great-grandmother was included in the margins and empty spaces as guideposts. She'd also tucked inside a slew of hand-written pages with instructions on using plants for medicinal purposes and the proper way to cast runes to divine the future.

I had recently learned that my eighth-removed great-grandmother was a renowned midwife and healer from the old country who'd escaped Salem during the time of the persecutions. *Mary Sarah Toogood.* And she'd brought these books on her back all the way to Canada during that difficult journey. To say I was proud to be her descendent was putting it mildly.

"We have need of guidance in protecting a loved one. Please speak through me and share with all what shall be done," I murmured to encourage the spirits to show me the best choices the book contained for our current situation.

When I didn't feel the pull to any specific page, I set the heavy book aside. "No guidance from the old ones today," I said with a sigh.

"That's good, right?" Tulip frowned, hovering by my side. "Means this won't be a problem."

"Maybe. It could also mean they're in a wait-and-see pattern. Maybe things are changing right now that we're unaware of."

"Like what?"

"I don't know, but when things are in a state of flux, the universe tends to hold its collective breath."

"Like, how do you know that for certain?" Star scoffed, tapping her toes on the tiled floor. "Could just mean you've lost your mojo, right?"

I declined to answer in efforts not to incriminate myself. I had to remind myself that my sister was not in her happy place, waiting around Snowy Lake, and that I really didn't want her to leave anyway.

"Serenity now," I whispered and turned my attention to the Northern Lights Coven grimoire with its eternity symbol captured in real gold flakes. Well, they looked like real gold, but their addition was thanks to Auntie T.J., which made them suspect. She has a habit of seeding Snowy Creek with fake nuggets to encourage tourists—not that we hadn't been a hotbed of treasure finds in decades past. A fact I was trying my best to ignore was that she-who-shall-not-be-mentioned AKA Jennifer pain-in-the-butt Morgan, an old girlfriend of Ace's and a geologist had found gold here again, and come spring, a whole commercial enterprise would be descending on our town.

Okay, time to concentrate.

I flipped carefully to the back where the more recent incantations had been added, thanks to me and the automatic writing that came over me on occasion, usually just before something was needed. And one to do with protection had been added a couple of days ago, meaning my *mojo* was just fine, thank you very much, Miss Star McCall.

The power of this particular grimoire to encourage the muses was legendary, even if it was a relatively modern tome. Granny Toogood's cursive writing had added a few incantations before she'd turned of age and lost her power. Apparently, her choice of mate hadn't quite lined up with the universe and its one-true-mate rule. Silly, and quite annoying, in my opinion. But, I supposed, it did keep one from sleeping around. Ever. *Rather a prissy universe.*

"So, which one?" Star asked. "You'd better choose quick because I can see Emma already coming down the street with Christine, followed by a few others." She had moved to the bay window, her attention divided.

"Hang on. Okay, this one jumps out at me," I said. I hated to be rushed. I could and did spend countless hours hunched over this living grimoire that held runes, sigils and protective amulets galore. A modern goddess' way of achieving her best life...and a *huge* challenge.

"Which one?" Tulip asked, peering over my shoulder.

"It's new. A protection spell."

The staccato stomping of high heels on the linoleum flooring coming ever closer made the hair on my neck rise.

I whirled around to see my roommate, Ivana Petrov, with her bright red Medusa hair, steely gray eyes and a brotherly connection that scared the stuffing right out of me. *Russian Bratva* was whispered by all the townspeople with a knowing nod. I'd give her one thing — she was great at making poppets to scare away interlopers or she-who-shall-not-be-mentioned. I swallowed hard and greeted her with my brightest smile.

"My friend. Why you not call? I take care of this matter for you. Hound Dog is problem, right?"

How had she found out? Either there was a leak in our coven or she'd sleuthed it out. I knew for certain I hadn't told her. "No worries. We've got this, but thanks so much. We're going with a protection spell from our grimoire. So, no need to involve yourself."

"Spell? *Phttt.* Russian answer better. More final," she said, batting her spectacular eyelashes.

"Ah, but it's for the best, my good friend. We need you to keep the big guns for more important matters. This" — I waved my arms about for emphasis — "is such small potatoes. Beneath you, really. I mean that, sincerely."

"Yes, I do have *big guns*." She smiled coyly while nodding. Today she was dressed in five-inch stilettos, a tight black skirt with a slit cut to mid-thigh, exposing fancy fishnet stockings, accompanied by a shocking pink sweater with a deeply plunging neckline that showed off those *big guns* admirably. The outfit made my throat dry. In my mind, I could see a blade strapped to one of those shapely thighs.

"Thank you, my friend. I'll call you if necessary. Have no fear of that." I moved forward to hug her. She did likewise, then pounded her chest over her heart with a fist. *Ooh, that had to hurt.*

"I am always for you," she said, then went to retrieve an éclair.

The door burst open and in trooped most of the Northern Lights Coven members. The world's finest cavalry had arrived.

Chapter Three

"What do you want us to do, Charm?" my best friend Emma Hurst asked, her sentiment echoed in tandem by my newest friend, Christine Blackmore. I was pleased to see Christine's belly had increased since I'd last seen her and how proud she looked in the tight stretchy top she wore that exposed it so admirably. She'd wanted a baby so badly that she'd turned to me for help. It had worked, and I prayed to the goddess daily that she and her hubby, Sean, would be blessed with a healthy newborn come springtime.

"I want each of you to read an incantation in sync to charge the blue agate locket filled with rosemary I'm going to have Auntie T.J. wear until further notice. It's perfect because it's in the shape of her spirit animal, the crow. Then we're going over to her house and lay protective measures. We'll use salt all around the outside of the house, spirits in the doorways and charge some bells with their mission to hang in the four corners."

"How about a loaded candle?"

"Can't hurt. Good idea, Emma. We'll burn one as well. Okay, Tulip, I need you to print this verse for everyone to chant." I handed her the parchment I had recently filled with the protection spell and pointed out the pertinent lines.

She hurried off and fired up her laptop and printer.

"I'd also like to do a Five Stone Protective Spell, but the dish needs to sit out to absorb the moonlight and starlight until sunrise, and I don't think Auntie T.J. can wait that long," I mused, considering the pros and cons while chewing on a thumbnail.

"I'll pick up the salt and spirits on the way over to her house. Eighty-proof whiskey okay?" Christine asked.

"That'll work great." I picked out the amulet that I wanted to charge from the display and took a few seconds to envision a pure blue light surrounding it.

"Here you go." Tulip pulled a stack of white pages from her printer and handed each of the twelve coven members who crowded the front of the café a printed slip of paper.

"Okay, everyone ready?" We didn't normally do this in such a rush, usually handwriting each incantation in cursive script, but I felt an impossible-to-resist urge to get it done. *Now.*

"Oh goddess, protect my loved one from harm, bathe her in your spirit and keep her strong. Help her repel any negative forces that a line against her, and give her the strength of your continued blessing. In the name of all the goddesses, we thank you," everyone recited in tandem.

"Okay, let's head over to her house," I said, picking up the four brass bells to be charged. "Oh, and grab an éclair to go. They're triple chocolate."

Star gave a deliberate eyeroll at my militarily precise tone. I considered giving *her* the bird, then decided to just usher everyone outside to hurry things along. I'd deal with her later. Maybe a spell to enact gratitude might be in order? *Just sayin'*.

The angel choir, AKA the wind chimes, spouted a chorus of tuneful glee that matched the four bells I held in my hands as our troop marched underneath, proof positive to my mind that we were on the correct path.

"Where y'all headed?" Constable Ace, a transplant originally from Kentucky, suddenly appeared at my side again, making me jump smartly in my skin. He was an expert at this maneuver. It had been a blessing and a curse. The curse was when I need some alone-sleuthing time when on a case — I was needed because of course I know my own people better than he ever could and get answers so much faster — otherwise, he was pretty much a blessing.

"Down to Telegraph Road to visit with Auntie T.J." Tegan Jane lived next to the library and had the most charming, gingerbread-style house in town.

"Uh-huh. And why are you carrying four noisy cow bells?" Ace's always delectable fragrance of manliness and outside freshness followed him like a happy entity. I filled my lungs with its steadying influence since we were standing so close. Well, most times it worked, but other moments it filled me with an unladylike antsy sensation that I wouldn't get into.

"We need them," I said with authority while I continued walking away at a fair clip.

"Yeah. What for?" He kept time with me on the sidewalk.

I shrugged, not meeting his eyes. "Just a little procedure we want to try."

"Using them to protect your aunt, by any chance?"

Ace is so darn well read that he rivaled yours truly when it came to an endless array of subjects he had a handle on — everything from the possibility of gifted humans with telepathy to the physics of quantum theory of time travel on a microscopic scale for wormholes. From Dean Radin to Carl Sagan. Often gifted to me. I go there as well, but I'm also a huge fan of Agatha Christie and collect all her books. A gal can never be too well-armed.

"Well, I want to talk to her as well. I intend to ask her to cease and desist, as per your request."

"Good. Glad we're on the same page, Miss McCall."

"Now when have we not been on the same page, Sheriff?" I asked, slanting my eyes at him. He wasn't an actual sheriff, but he did give off the vibe of a man prepared for a *High Noon* situation at any given moment. Was it my imagination or did the bells ring one hundred percent louder?

Not often enough. And this darn town's always trying to keep us apart.

"Did you say something?"

"Nope. You must be hearing things." Ace removed his hat and smoothed down his thick hair before placing his headgear back on at a winning angle.

"Hmm. Well, I've taken up enough of your time, Sheriff. I'll just be moseying along."

"There was something else. I hear you've been busy preparing for the Sadie Hawkins dance?"

We'd reached the end of Main Street by this time and had turned north onto Telegraph Road, following the troop of coven members marching ahead of us and chattering like magpies.

"Yes, that's what I do. Well, one of my jobs anyway. What are you getting at, Sheriff?"

I gave him a quick look and noted his skin color had deepened under his tan. "I was wondering if you had a date or anything, you know, for the dance?"

"I guess you don't know how a Sadie Hawkins dance works, eh?" I said, pressing my lips together to keep the broad smile wanting to take my lips hostage from becoming too obvious.

"What do you mean?" He turned my way those devasting whiskey-brown eyes of his that a woman could sink right into and forget to breathe.

"Sadie Hawkins is code for 'the woman invites the man'."

"What? Since when?"

"Since like forever." My bet was that he knew this but was hedging for some reason. "The idea was hatched by the Lil' Abner comic strip created by Al Capp that ran in November 1937. The unmarried women of Dogpatch got to chase the bachelors and 'marry up' with the ones that they caught. You lookin' to get caught, Sheriff?"

Gotcha. His skin turned a deeper and even more becoming shade of red.

I hurried to have my say before he stomped off. It looked imminent. "For your information, no, I don't have a date for the dance. But I was wondering, if you have the night free, if you would consent to be my date?"

"You lookin' to catch and release, darlin', or catch and keep?"

I swallowed, riveted by the tall Mountie who strolled by my side like he owned the entire world and so effectively took my mind away from any other thought of late.

"Looks like we're arrived," he added.

"What?" I gawked over at Auntie T.J.'s front yard from the sidewalk. "Right! Well, thank you for the escort. I'll take it from here."

He saluted with that two-finger slide of his hat brim he had going for him before adding a dashing smile. "Later."

"Maybe."

He turned back. "One other thing, I've been reading a book on grimoires, *A History of Magic Books* by Owen Davies that I think you might like to borrow."

"What made you chose that one?"

He shrugged. "A whim. And I know the subject interests you. It's pretty good, mentions those books your eighth-removed great-grandmother brought across the border in the seventeenth century."

"What do you know about our magic books?" I narrowed my eyes at him.

"More than you think, darlin'. I'll drop it off later."

"I may or may not be home," I challenged.

"Oh, you'll be home all right. There's a spell for that if you're not." The bright light in his eyes eclipsed the sun.

"Why, Constable Ace Collins, if I didn't know better—"

"So, we doing this or what?" Star asked, suddenly right in my face. "She's not home, so if we hurry, we can get everything in place before she comes back."

I sighed and counted to ten. "Yes, we are. Lead the way."

I ignored the speculative glances I received from the coven and hurried to direct the necessary actions to protect Auntie's house. "Okay, Emma, you pour the salt all around the house. Christine, does the smell of spirits bother you?"

"A bit."

"Okay, Tulip, you anoint the doorways. I'll instruct the bells and then we can all get together and offer up the prayer."

Emma joined me, giving me a sideways glance as she took three of the bells from me so I could hook one to the southern-east corner of Auntie's living room. "I heard about the altercation between your aunt and the Hound Dog this morning. You okay?"

I shrugged, struggling to reach the golden plant holder that worked admirably as a protective bell depositor. "Sure. It's just suddenly Ling Ling announces a ghost, Tulip observes a devil face in the sky and my auntie is acting like she's five years old. I know, I should be used to it by now, but some days—"

"I guess it doesn't help that your mother's coming back to town." Emma's sweet, freckled face framed by red curls blurred for a second. I dropped the bell, making the whole coven give a collective gasp. Taking a deep breath, I worked to steady myself. "I'd better recharge it."

"Sorry. I didn't mean to upset you. I'm here for you, whenever you need to talk. You know that."

"No worries. Everything happens for a reason, right?" I had my doubts about the upcoming visit by a woman I hadn't seen since she'd unceremoniously dumped my sisters and I at the age of eight, but... *Miracles happen, right?*

"Okay, join hands," I instructed. "Sacred bell, I beg your forgiveness for dropping you, and ask in the name of the goddess that you protect anyone who resides in this house by warning them of harm. In the name of the Northern Lights Coven, I thank you for your service."

The incantation finished, I added, "Okay, let's get the other three in place then find out where Auntie T.J.

is so we can give her the protection amulet. She's out there undefended."

"She was last seen at the library," Star said. "Miriam said she left ten minutes ago, and she was on her way to Skull Cave."

"Skull Cave." My heart thudded. "Please, please don't let her run into Sergei," I muttered and took a deep breath. "Okay, let's go. Whose vehicle is closest?"

"Mine's outside," Emma said. "When I stopped with Christine to pick up the whiskey, I insisted on driving us here." She leaned down and whispered in my ear, "She was looking a tad peaked."

"Of course. Okay, let's go."

"I call shotgun," Star spoke up.

"No, you and Tulip wait here. I got this." I turned to my fellow coven members. "Thanks for coming and helping. No one has our backs more than the Northern Lights. It means a lot to me and my family."

"You're kidding, right! Tulip and I are both coming, so you can just deal with it, Charm. She's our auntie too." Star's voice rose over the leave-taking of the other women.

Tulip nodded her head vigorously. "I'm going too."

"Okay, fine, but the pair of you ride in the back."

"What's the point of sayin' 'shotgun' if it doesn't count for anything?" Star muttered.

"You are *not* five years old anymore."

"*Phttt*. Some things don't have a statute of limitations attached."

I ignored the dig as we left the house and walked down the sidewalk to where Emma had parked her white Ford Explorer at the curb. "Star, I need you to focus right now. Could you do that, please? I have a sense that something's not right. Too many ominous signs today. We need to pull together, now more than ever."

Star had the grace to look contrite. "Yes, of course. For our auntie, I can focus. You just had to say, you know."

We had reached the vehicle and we all piled in. I was antsy to get going. I had not been understating my feeling that something was off. *Totally.* All my senses churned along at a mile-a-minute, nearly spinning out of control. I was hard-pressed not to stomp hard on the gas pedal as Emma chastely signaled before pulling out carefully into non-existent traffic. I bit my tongue instead. *Ouch.*

Chapter Four

Skull Cave was near Spirit Springs, on the eastern side of the lake our town was named after and down a spectacularly bumpy logging road that had been somewhat improved when the movie company had filmed a few weeks earlier—the movie company that was threatening to take my sister away any day now. Though I had come to grips with the changes, a part of me still hoped the deal fell through. *Does that make me a bad person? Wanting to keep my family close?*

I had no time to dwell on the ethics of the thing because we were suddenly accosted by Auntie T.J.'s cherry-red Volkswagen headed full-tilt in our direction.

"Watch out!" I shouted, yanking the steering wheel toward me and away from Emma who was driving and looking like she was about to lose it. I was hoping to head the Explorer for a near miss or the ditch.

As the Bug swept by us, going a gazillion miles an hour over the speed limit, leaving us at least physically intact and still on the actual roadway, a police siren began to pierce the air close by. I swiveled my head around and spied Ace on our tail, then watched as he made a superb U-turn that he would have called me out for and begin to chase after Auntie T.J.

"Get after them, Emma!" I shouted.

Emma gave me a dropped-chin look that didn't flatter, shaking her head. "I'm about done in, Charm. Could you take over?"

I jumped right over her and into the driver's seat as she slid under me and onto the passenger side in one spectacular stunt move worthy of Catwoman. There was a double gasp from the back seat that I ignored as I pushed the gas pedal to the metal and spun the vehicle around on its rubber, heading back the way we came.

On the edge of the town proper, we came across Auntie T.J., now pulled over, and Ace getting out of his SUV. A very grim look stiffened his face and made me nervous.

I jumped out of the Ford and raced to join the action.

"What's going on? Auntie, are you okay?" I asked, hurrying to her side and ignoring the Mountie who I knew one hundred percent for certain could take care of himself. Other than my auntie's curls looking askew and her lipstick smeared, she looked intact, nothing obvious broken.

She waved my inquiry aside, breathing deeply. "I'm fine. Don't fuss."

"What's going on, Miss Toogood?" Ace asked. "You were driving double the speed limit posted for this road. You could have hurt someone driving like that." His tone held a great deal of supressed anger, and I realized he'd been worried, observing our near-miss on the roadway.

I pulled the talisman jewelry from my pocket, giving Ace a cease-and-desist look that I hoped he understood. "Here. I'm putting this on you. It will protect you from harm."

"I think you're better off putting that around your own neck," Ace said, his tone as sharp as the creases in his immaculate uniform pants. He turned to my aunt. "Tell me what happened to have you driving so recklessly. Keep in mind your answer better be forthcoming or I will be doing my sworn duty and hauling you off to the detachment forthwith."

"Ah, I saw something."

I saw the moment she found a solution and inwardly groaned.

"A ghost. It was chasing me and I tried to outrun it. That's all. It will never happen again, Officer. I promise." Auntie T.J. made the sign of a cross over her heart. "Say, what's your plan for Sadie Hawkins?" My incorrigible aunt batted her thickly mascaraed eyelashes at Ace.

"A ghost?" I narrowed my eyes at her. She was lying through her teeth.

Ace turned a deep red and that darn tic began under his right eye. "You don't endanger other people over a ghost supposedly chasing you. What really happened?"

"You do if said ghost is carrying a scythe. Since you have no plans, I'm officially asking you to the Sadie Hawkins dance as my guest."

"Ace has plans. I've already asked him and he said yes. Now, about that ghost. Whose ghost was it? Baby Ling Ling talked about seeing one earlier."

"The ghost that guards the treasure of Gold Mountain."

"You were after treasurer? And what do you mean, Ling Ling told you about one earlier?" Ace asked, his expression beyond perplexed, flitting his gaze back and forth between my auntie and myself. *This might be a good time to beat it.*

"Auntie's not been feeling well lately. I think I should get her home. No real harm done, right? You don't want to put an old lady in the hoosegow, do you, Sheriff? Remember what happened when you arrested me?" The coven members had hoisted a burning effigy of Constable Ace Collins on the detachment lawn to protest my unlawful detainment. *And rightly so.*

"I have not been party to the facts of any local treasure legend. Would one of you like to tell me what's really going on here?"

"Just what I said. According to legend, a man was murdered near Gold Mountain over the rightful owner of a gold claim by his partner. That's all there is to it, Officer. And today when I walked through that area over on — ah — the backside of one of the tributaries that run into Snowy River that carries gold down from the mountain, I was accosted by his ghost. Probably on a walk-a-bout."

"And he was carrying a scythe on his shoulder?"

"Yup, a very sharp-looking one." My auntie shuddered theatrically.

"Huh." Ace took off his Stetson, smoothed down his hair and carefully placed his hat on again. "I know I'm going to regret this, but I am going to let you go with a stern warning and a promise from you to never go over the speed limit again. From you too, Miss McCall."

"What? I wasn't speeding nearly half as much."

"So you admit you were driving over the posted limit?"

"Fine, I promise to drive more carefully. Auntie?"

She had a mulish look on her face that rivaled her niece Star's best performance.

"Auntie!"

"Okay, okay, I promise. Cheez, see how you do with an armed ghost coming after you. I'll bet you'd hightail it out of there in a squeal of rubber."

"And if I catch either of you breaking the law for the next five years, I'll be adding this incident to the charge. Consider yourselves on probation."

"What! That's not fair. It was my auntie who started this whole thing."

"Suck it up, buttercup!" Auntie T.J cackled with glee.

I slanted my eyes and could definitely see her stirring a cauldron filled with vile concoctions at some point in history. *A cauldron I am about ready to toss her bony hiney into.*

"Are we free to leave?" I asked, clenching my jaw so tightly that it made a cracking sound. *Serenity now.*

"You okay?" Ace asked.

"I'm fine. Thanks for not throwing her in jail." I remembered my manners in the nick of time. The excellent training from Granny Toogood often came to the rescue.

"You're welcome. I'll be watching you both." He strode off and got back into his RCMP SUV. He didn't drive away immediately but sat and waited.

"What really happened?" I spoke furiously under my breath, leaning in close to the culprit and trying to stay out of the sight line of the Mountie.

"Nothing. Do you know where Ivana Petrov is?"

"Ivana? What do you want her for?"

"Not like you're going to have my back. I need her help is all."

My heart sank into my shoes. "What kind of help?"

"You know that old saying about knowing if you've got a really good friend if they help you with certain kinds of things with no questions asked?"

"What have you done, now?" I rubbed at my forehead, hoping she was joking with the possible 'burying-the-body' reference.

"Oh my, I need a drink."

"Later. Hold out your hands. I want a reading on this. Think about what happened today."

"No way! You're not pulling that voodoo trick on me." Her lips thinned and she backed up a few feet. That was beyond strange. I had helped Auntie find a number of lost items doing that exact same maneuver.

"Fine. But you know I'll be checking this out now, right? Where were you just now? Skull Cave? Because I know you were lying your butt off to Ace." I was fairly certain I'd find mason jars filled with Apple Pie Moonshine in her locked truck, but I couldn't take the chance on looking and drawing attention to her illegal activities. *Did I mention that Ace is a real straight shooter?*

"Don't do that. Ghosts are nothing to scoff at. Why, to think I changed your diapers, missy, and this is the thanks I get."

"Auntie, you are aware that we arrived in Snowy Lake when all of us were eight, right?" We'd had this discussion before.

"Figure of speech. Now, I'm headed home. I suggest you do the same. The law's got us in their sites." She made the gesture of two fingers over her eyes then directed them at Ace, who was still watching us watch him. He was on his radio now, his attention hopefully getting directed elsewhere.

I needed a reading on my aunt, and I needed it now. Racing after the woman hotfooting it for her vehicle, I caught her at the driver's door. "If you got nothing to hide, why won't you let me get a reading on what happened?"

The siren on Ace's SUV blasted off and he made another U-turn before driving carefully by the two of us, then he gunned the motor and headed back in the direction of Spirits Springs and Skull Cave.

"Auntie! Last chance. What happened?" But she was already moving quicker than I thought her capable of, buckling up behind the wheel of her Ladybug, as she called her Volkswagen, then driving away toward town in a squeal of burning rubber.

I raced back to the Ford Explorer and jumped in.

"What's going on?" came a chorus of chirps that I ignored as I spun the vehicle on a dime and took off after Ace, who was already a cloud of dust in the distance.

Chapter Five

"Charm! Answer us. Why is Auntie going one way and we're following Constable Ace the other way?" Star shouted above the din.

"Shoot! I should have told her to stay away from Ivana." I hit the steering wheel with the palm of my hand. "Ouch."

"What? Why does your auntie want to see Ivana?" Emma asked, turning a horrified glance my way. My best friend was petrified of Ivana.

"I don't know." I couldn't very well say what I suspected so shrugged, feeling a nervous tic of my own announce itself under my left eye, firing off like lightning bug did at dusk as I fished around for an answer. "Maybe to gift her some of her famous moonshine."

"Tell us what you know now, Charm, or so help-me-goddess, I'm going straight to Granny with this." The threat came from Star, of course.

"All I know is that Auntie T.J. said she saw a ghost holding a scythe, got frightened and scurried back to town. Then Ace got a call on his radio and took off. So, we're following to find out why. Okay? That's it, you're up to date."

"Did you take a reading on her? Put the charmed talisman around her neck?" Tulip asked.

"No to the first question and yes to the second. We can all breathe easier, as she's better protected."

"What? That's crazy about her not letting you take a reading. You were just trying to help her with the scary ghost situation." Emma appeared scandalized that my auntie had refused the offer. "You could figure out whose ghost it is, right, and fix things?"

"Thanks, Emma, that's exactly what I would have tried to do." Not that I was an expert on seeing ghosts. But how hard could it be to figure out what they wanted? *Just ask.*

We were now at the parking lot that led to springs and the cave beyond. I parked Emma's Ford beside the police SUV. We'd have to hoof it the rest of the way.

I clambered out, and with the other three hard on my heels, we scurried after Ace, headed down the gravel path for Spirit Springs. The mist rose like ghostly fingers over the heated medicinal water as we trooped on by. I kept my eyes on the prize — Ace still striding well ahead of us. I suspected he knew we were hot on his tail, and my suspicions were confirmed when at the cave's entrance he stopped and waited for us to catch up.

He pursed his lips, his glance more steely-eyed then I had ever seen it. "I'm going to have to ask all of you to wait here. This is official police business. You go inside, and I will have to detain you. Are we clear?"

I swallowed, my stomach roiling like I had boarded an ailing ship in a storm. "What's going on? Did someone report a crime?"

"I am responding to a call. I will tell you more when I am able. Wait here." He turned and strode off.

We huddled together. "You got any bars on your phone, Star?" Of the four of us, Star was most likely to have cell phone reception.

"No, darn it." She gave that famous pout. I was torn between driving back to town and waiting to see what Ace had to say.

I dithered, chewing on my thumbnail again. Then footfalls alerted us to company coming our way. We moved in closer to the entrance.

It wasn't Ace coming back, but a former beau of Granny Toogood's and our man-stealing auntie. The man had almost caused a rift between the pair years ago, and I used this as a direct threat to keep auntie in line when necessary. *Looks like it might be time to haul out the big guns to get her to cooperate.* Though in truth, I prayed that Granny would never hear of it. *Imagine, on New Year's Eve, bedding the man in a back room of a dance hall?*

I narrowed my eyes at the culprit I silently referred to as Tweedy Bird, due to his insistence on wearing the fabric overmuch. "Sylvester Byrd. What are you doing here?"

"None of your business, missy," he hissed. He hung around the entrance, making me even more suspicious. Had he and auntie been having another tryst? Was that why she wouldn't let me have a go at her? I gritted my teeth.

More footsteps and another man joined Tweedy. Gerald McCleod. *What's he doing here?*

"Mr. Byrd, what do you know about what's going on?" Star asked, batting her eyes at him. "We're all a little concerned is all." She shrugged. "My auntie was upset when we saw her a few minutes ago, and we know how very much you care about her."

"Tegan Jane's upset?" He used her full name. "I had nothing to do with that. I was the one who found the body, not her. Well, me and Gerald here."

Gerald nodded. He had a reputation as being a quiet man, one he lived up to.

"What! You found a body. Where?"

"None of your business. I'm not supposed to be talking to you anyway. Constable said to keep it to myself. He'll be out here directly. Ask him for yourself. Not like he's capable of hiding much from you, since you caught his eye. Whole town's talking about the pair of you. If you ask my opinion, I say let the chips fall as they may. I don't believe you can heal anyone anyway. All that hocus pocus is bull malarkey."

"Listen, buster, *spill* or there will be consequences." I was stepping out on a limb without a net, but a sense of everything going sideways pushed hard. I needed to regain control of this. *Now.* Halloween was right around the corner, meaning chaos would descend if the town didn't have its ducks in a row beforehand. *2017.* The year that would live in infamy when the self-designated Hatfields and McCoys had pushed the envelope to the brink of ruin and nearly brought back the dead. It had only been an intervention by the entire Northern Lights Coven that had saved the town by a costly array of protection spells that had had to be manned day and night. I shuddered at the memory.

"I don't have to tell you *anything*." Tweedy Bird's ears grew darker. "Just wait until your mother comes back and then we'll know for certain what's going on."

"Know what for certain about what?"

"All I'm going to say on the matter." He zipped his hand across his mouth and shut down, standing mutely beside the statue that was Gerald McCleod.

"What's he talking about? What's our mother got to do with all this?"

"I don't know, Tulip." I have her a sideways hug because she looked so forlorn, kicking at the gravel with the toe of her tennis shoe, scuffing the rubber and canvas. I had to remind myself that the sad memories of my sibling rivaled mine. Nothing good had happened before we were eight and had come into Granny Toogood's care. *Well, maybe being born.* "I guess we'll have to wait and see."

Taking a deep breath, I made an instant decision. "Okay, enough of this. I'm going in." Before anyone could object, I headed into my least favorite place on earth. The oppressive landform that I had only recently come to grips with during the movie shoot when I had found a pair of very ill stuntmen then saved their lives, according to Doc Stone.

I did my best to ignore the otherworldly sensation that the weird sheets of calcite flowing down the ancient walls caused, and instead focused on where Ace was. Slight noises in the distance aided my search and the pot lighting newly installed by the movie people helped even further.

"Cheez, if only I knew an invisibility spell that worked," I muttered to keep up my flagging courage as I picked my way through the dripping pools of acidic water that had helped form stalactites that were now pointed downward. *Right at me.*

"But wouldn't that entail using modern metamaterials, electrical and optical engineering and the geometry of curved space? Einstein's theory of general relativity and Maxwell's principles of electromagnetism combined. Hmm, maybe it's time to consult the older grimoires?" It sounded easier that finding metamaterials or getting a university degree. That idea upped my confidence, and I strode forward with more purpose.

Then around a bend in the rockface, I came face to face with Sergei McCausland lying prone on the ground, a Mason jar still clutched in his right hand. The distinctive scent of Apple Pie Moonshine wafted about the small enclave. Was he drunk? Passed out?

The side space also held a few jugs of the alcohol, lined up. I knew his moonshine was somewhere else in the cave system, well hidden from prying eyes. This was a waystation only, a place where he sold his product to cave visitors. The cave system had a number of underground streams, supplying the necessary H2O to make the distilled liquor, a deciding factor, no doubt, in him having chosen the dismal location. A moonshiner couldn't very well house the illegal activity in their own basement, drawing unwanted attention.

"What are you doing?" Ace turned on me, his handsome mug on lockdown, held hostage by a scowl.

"Coming to help. What's going on? Sergei passed out?"

His lips were in danger of disappearing. "No. The man is deceased. I need you to stay back. Do you understand, Miss McCall? Nod if you do."

I nodded, realizing I was too late to help. What had happened? I badly wanted to touch the mason jar and get a reading, find out who had recently handled it. The fragrance of the corn whiskey saturated the air, the fumes making me dizzy. I glanced at Sergei again, noting his bluish color. How long had he been dead? I had seen him alive just a few short hours ago when Auntie had accosted him. *Oh boy*. Was this somehow related? Was that why Auntie was lying about her whereabouts and looking for help from Ivana, of all people? Was Tweedy Bird being here just a coincidence?

"Are you sure I can't help him?" I chewed on a fingernail since my thumbnail was decimated, wishing I could at least try. Sergei might be a womanizer and a whole host of other things, but no one wished him dead. Or did they? Was this why the universe had been stirring me up this morning?

"No, he's gone. Sorry. Did you know him well?" Ace looked up from his inspection of the area surrounding the body.

"Not well. My family didn't get along—" Then I realized the words would incriminate us if indeed foul play had gone on.

"I gathered that this morning when your aunt serenaded the man. Now, I can't get reception on my cell. Could you go back to the entrance and call the sheriff for me? Tell him it's urgent."

"Okay. I can do that." I badly wanted to stay but could think of no legitimate excuse.

When I hesitated, he gave me another look from under his awesome hat and I turned around, fleeing the scene.

I found everyone still crowded around the cave's entrance.

"Star, do you have reception now?"

"Yeah. I just sent a text that worked. What's going on?"

"Ace found something, and he needs Winn Duffy to come out."

"So, there is a body. Whose is it?" She worked the phone with her thumbs as she spoke. Then she talked to the detachment receptionist, telling her to send the sheriff.

"Sergei McCausland."

Tweedy Bird was ignoring all of us, working his own phone, looking beyond frustrated. *Good luck with that.* Star was the only one with the juice to make a cell phone work at this distance from the tower.

The sound of another siren coming from town drew our attention.

"I'm going to head back."

"I'm coming with you," Emma said and soon all four of us were hurrying back the way we'd come.

I whispered out of the side of my mouth, "Let me handle this."

It was Sunday. If the sheriff was in evidence, this added a whole lot of credibility that there was something huge going on, meaning Ace suspected more than just a natural death, considering how much the man loved his wife's home cooking and should be home enjoying it. I checked my watch. One o'clock. *Yup, lunch time.*

My stomach gave a gurgle of agreement.

"Sheriff, just the man I wanted to see."

"What is it, Charm? I'm in a hurry here." His face was flushed from the quick pace he'd set. I about-faced and kept military stride with him, beginning to feel like I was well into an episode of the Keystone Cops.

"I was wondering if there's anything you can share about what's going on? Granny Toogood's worried and I want to reassure her." I felt a bit bad playing the trump card, especially so early on in an investigation, but the need to know ate at me. Most likely the Hound Dog had been murdered. Otherwise, why had the universe brought me out here and been sending me messages all morning? It was hardly business as usual.

"Granny has no need to worry. I'm just here to help Ace investigate."

We were nearly back to the cave entrance now and I was desperate for answers.

"Is Doc Tanner on the way?" He sometimes doubled as our medical examiner or at least recognized if we needed to call in bigger guns.

"Best you stay out of it," he said not unkindly. "Now, I advise all of you to head off home and keep this to yourselves."

Tweedy Bird began to move faster than the rest of us.

"Ah, not you, Mr. Byrd. I need to talk to you. You wait here." And Sheriff Winn Duffy entered the cave, leaving us to stew outside.

"Okay." I let out a deep breath. "We might as well head home for now."

Emma's eyebrows were MIA under her curly red bangs, her eyes owl-like again. "Did you see him? Sergei?"

"I did. He'd been drinking Apple Pie Moonshine just before he died." *Probably what killed him. Please, let it be his own pirated version.* The uncomfortable thoughts flashed through my brain. "And we'd better hurry and check on Auntie T.J. ASAP. She has some explainin' to do."

Chapter Six

With most of Snowy Lake's lawmen out at Skull Cave, we drove back to town unmolested, heavy-footed as I was. *Not my fault.* I was wound up, between the probable murder case, Auntie's odd behavior, Halloween right around the corner and talk of my mother coming back to town. I needed a dirty martini like a panda bear needed bamboo. I parked in front of the Tea & Tarot and shut off the motor.

"Let's split up and look for Auntie T.J. I'll check in with Granny and see if she knows anything."

"I'll swing by her house on the way home." Emma volunteered. "She's probably safe and sound, sitting among all those protection spells."

"Star and I will scout the town for anyone who's seen her," Tulip said.

"Good. *Oh shoot*, Homecoming's this Friday and we've got to start baking."

Homecoming was always the day before the Sadie Hawkins dance, and we prepared all the desserts. How could I have forgotten? Most people just hung around for both events, which made the town pretty busy all weekend, but the next week was Halloween, All Hallows' Eve. Then Samhain, when the veil thinned between the worlds and more things are possible than met the eye. My absolute favorite celebration...if I got this mess resolved in time. And it fell on a Saturday night with a full moon this year. Could there have been a more perfect storm for trying some brand-new alchemy?

"I'll help and round up some of the Northern Lights who're free," Emma said. She earned a wide grin from me.

"Perfect. Thank you."

I headed into the café, and, finding no one in restaurant section, headed into the kitchen. "Granny! How are you?"

Granny Toogood was sitting at the small table we used for our breaks, holding a rose-patterned teacup between her hands. She looked up and gave me a wan smile, her face paler than usual. My heart stuttered and I rushed to her side. I crouched down on the floor beside her and laid my hand on her arm.

"What is it? What's wrong?"

"Charm. Sit down, sweeting. I have something I must share with you."

Kissing her soft cheek, I made myself get up and take a seat across from her. I swallowed. "Okay. I'm ready. What is it?"

"I dread telling you this, knowing how talk of your mother upsets you, but there's nothing else to be done. Your mother's very ill. Her kidneys have shut down, probably due to all those years of doing drugs and drinking." Granny shook her head, looking older than

I had ever seen her. "She's coming home in a few days to see all of you. It's her last wish — to try to make things right with you and your sisters."

Horrified, I sat and tried to take in the information. I wanted to scream, to throw my body onto the floor in a tantrum like Star had been notorious for doing when she was two years old, but I couldn't seem to move my paralyzed limbs.

"I know this must be very upsetting for you. It's a lot to take in." Granny reached across the table and laid her hard-working, blue-veined hands on mine. Tears prickled behind my eyelids and I swallowed against the large lump that was suddenly threatening to cut off my breathing tube. *Just. Breathe.*

"What does she want, really?" Thirteen years she had ignored all of us, and now she wanted to come home to die? *To make things right? No.* That wasn't possible.

"I think she just wants to see you all one last time. Apparently, she's been on an organ transplant list for some time, but she's pretty much given up."

"And she wants one of us to give her a part of our body, right? Just so she can destroy it again with drugs and alcohol? If that's what she wants, she can just stay away." I shook my head, then wiped the tears that had fallen off my chin. I thought I was all cried out about my past. I guessed that had never really happened. Being abandoned so young will always suck.

Granny shook her head, making her white curls move softly. Those curls that had gone even whiter, it seemed, overnight. "I don't think that's her intention."

"Where's she going to live?"

"With Auntie T.J."

"Oh, Auntie T.J." I bit the inside of my cheek hard, drawing blood. At least Star and Tulip wouldn't have to live with a woman they didn't want to be around. But we'd all be pressed into seeing her at some point. *Too small a town to avoid it.* Was I capable of handling it like an adult? My mind shied away from even being able to give it a proper think, my thoughts in such turmoil over what her coming back home would mean for all of us. How it could set us all back. Make us relive the most awful times of our lives. Freezing and hungry, for days on end. Locked in a cupboard, in the dark.

The bad memories threatened to overwhelm, and I tried putting a barrier to the past up in my mind. *Stop it!* I wanted to scream, but with Granny sitting across from me, I had to hold it together. The woman deserved the best. Then a reminder of events from this morning came back to me. Something to hold on to. I sat up straighter. *Focus on what you can do well, Charm.* "You don't know what happened."

"What is it, sweeting?"

"A body was just found out at Skull Cave. The Hound—Sergei McCausland's dead."

"The man my sister was serenading this morning on Main Street?"

"Yes, ma'am, the very one. A mason jar of Apple Pie Moonshine was in his hand."

Granny frowned. Her blues eyes filled with an otherworldly intelligence. "He pirated her recipe and my sister's pretty upset about it. What do you think happened?"

"I'm looking into it. Ah, she wouldn't let me take a reading off her to clear her and show me what she knew." *I can make this work—just keep moving forward.* That was the key.

"No? That is odd. She's hiding something. But your aunt's no killer."

"Of course not, but it looks bad. Everyone's out looking for her right now. We put a few protection spells on her house, well, before this happened."

"Good. That will help. You know, I noticed an old camper on a truck bed over at the Bowl-a-ram-a parking lot earlier this morning. I wonder if there's any connection? I thought it strange, as normally Sergei doesn't allow people to park there. Says he's no freewheeling Wally World that allows people to park overnight."

"I'll look into it. Any idea where Auntie T.J. is?"

Granny shook her head. "Maybe she's gone back home. Charm, are you going to be all right? I hated to drop all this on you."

"Not your fault. I'll be fine." *Act like I'm fine until I am, right?*

"You don't have to always be the strong one, you know. You've taken so much on yourself, seeing to your sisters. You had to grow up so fast. It breaks my heart."

"We were the lucky ones. We had you, Granny." Speaking my truth made me feel better. More capable of staying away from the dark side...our childhood.

Her soft blue eyes filled with tears, so I jumped up and gave her an impulsive hug and kissed her cheek. "Now, I'm off. The Northern Lights will probably be by today to help with the desserts for Homecoming, so don't be worrying about that. It's all covered. Emma's on it."

"If Emma's on it then it's as good as done."

We shared a smile and I hurried out of the back door to retrieve Thor, my handy Jeep Cherokee that I had

obtained for a year of free desserts to the previous owner. I wanted to check all the usual haunts, leaving the next visit to Skull Cave until nightfall so I could procure an item I was certain would help me with the investigation. I needed to know everyone else who had seen the Hound Dog today. Someone had wished him ill — well, a lot of people had wished him ill, but only one had wanted him dead. Okay, that was another maybe. I shook my head. But what could he expect when the whole town called him the Hound Dog?

Driving past the Bowl-a-ram-a, I took note of the camper Granny Toogood had spoken of. I turned Thor's wheel to the right and parked beside the beat-up old truck that was set back from the business and half-hidden by an old oak tree. Granny had good eyes.

I rapped loudly on the metal door of the dingy yellow camper. There were few vehicles in the lot, most of them huddled right up near the front door of the white-clad business. Over the doorway was the flashing neon Bowl-a-ram-a sign with the constantly falling down and cheery getting right-back-up-again bowling pins. I'd admired those pins for years. It was my favorite part of the business. *Perfect strikes every two seconds. If only life were like that.* A flashback to my recent conversation with Granny made me rap even louder on the door the second time. There was still no answer.

I tried the doorknob and the camper door swung right open at my touch, revealing a body lying on the postage-stamp-sized carpeted floor.

Oh. My. Goddess. Was that a mason jar of Apple Pie Moonshine spilled and soaking the world's dingiest carpeting? The strong odor permeated the stifling air, stronger than at Skull Cave due to the lack of space.

There was barely room for one adult to maneuver around, let alone two. But I was going to try.

I climbed inside and closed the door. This was my one chance to see if any clues were left, and I wasn't going to blow it by calling in the law too quickly. Snowy Lake was my town, and I had every right to protect my own, to get the job done. A sudden image of the RCMP badge I had a friend make a couple of months back and that Ace had confiscated appeared. *Well, no fear. It's not the badge that matters — it's the intention, right?* And my intentions were to clear Auntie T.J., with or without her help, and nail the real culprit.

The body of the man took up most of the floor space — a youngish-looking man, which made it all that much more tragic. It was obvious he was dead. His skin tone had gone blue and the lack of life in his wide-open unblinking eyes chilled me to the marrow. I couldn't bring back the dead, as much as I wished it. I made myself lay two fingers against the side of his cold neck just to be certain. There was no pulse, but I jumped back when a snap of electricity shot up my arm. *What was that?*

Normally only the living could share their thought images with me. Was this a strange version of necromancy? To my understanding, though, it was the art of divination via the dead. The dead did not actually have to be in attendance. I would have preferred a Ouija board, holding a séance or even having a dream over having the corpse present, though.

"So, what do you want to tell me, sir?" Okay, I have no fancy words for this, no memorized spells and definitely no experience working with the newly departed. I gathered myself and tried again. Less power bit into me this time, but still some energy remained. I closed my eyes to see if that would help, if some image might make the leap into my mind.

A darkness invaded my soul and I shuddered, but I made myself hold on to the dead man. An image appeared, half out of focus, then clearer as I allowed it to enter my mind. It looked like a map. An old-fashioned treasure map with an X marking the spot. *Hand drawn*. The image faded and I sat back on my heels.

"Where was it? In the camper?"

No answer.

I got up and began to snoop. Well, it was in my job description. And who else would have just talked to the dead about a treasure map? Nothing obvious rose out of the mess that greeted my eyes. Old takeout bags, chocolate-bar wrappers, used tissue—*eww*, and dirty clothes. I desperately wanted to don plastic gloves for a thorough search. Was there time for that? To go home and get hand sanitizer as well? *Not likely.*

I did the next best thing, envisioned my immune system as being on its highest setting ever and waded in. Fifteen minutes later, I had found nothing of interest. Whoever had done the deed had taken every bit of incriminating evidence with them. Well, except for the mason jar of moonshine which was planted front and center and likely meant to be found.

A sudden, explosive rap at the camper's only door sent my heart into a wheeling skid and I gasped. I placed one hand on my chest and looked around frantically for a place to hide. Nothing jumped at me. No nice escape hatch like Howard the accountant had had on his RV out at the movie set…the RV where he'd gotten himself done in twice. I shook my head. That had been some feat.

Well, just have to brave it out.

I opened the door…and came face to face with Constable Ace Collins. *Natch.* A sense of déjà vu made my heart skitter. Maybe it was time to rethink my modus operandum? Being up close and personal to the virile man also wasn't helping a bit.

Chapter Seven

"Hi," I said, sharing my brightest smile ever. "I was just coming to get you."

His steely-eyed assessment just made me show more teeth.

"Aw, if you could move to the side, I'll be on my way. Leave you to do your job, Sheriff."

"What are *you* doing here?"

"Granny mentioned she'd seen the camper earlier, and we thought I'd best check on things. Be neighborly and give them a big Snowy Lake welcome. In my defense, I had no idea something untoward had happened."

"He's dead, isn't he." It wasn't a question, but an accusation.

"Yup, looks like it. I should be going. You haven't seen Auntie T.J. by any chance? I'm needing her help preparing desserts for the Homecoming dinner."

"No, I have not. How long have you been in here, Miss McCall?"

"You mean in the camper?" I cannot tell a lie well — one of my weaknesses — and especially not to Ace. Perhaps it had something to do with his being possibly my one? I tried to edge around him, but he was having none of it, blocking the doorway with his Bigfoot-sized body.

"Yes, in the camper. Well?" His glance pinned me in place, and I swallowed. Would it be inappropriate to lean forward a couple of inches and kiss him?

"A few minutes." Oh, what if I'd touched the last body? Would I discover a connection between the deaths? I fairly itched to find out if it were true. My face must have given me away, because Ace heaved out a pronounced put-upon sigh.

"What did you find out? And no holding out on me, Miss McCall, you hear me?"

"Could we talk outside? It's a bit tight in here." *Not to mention awkward.*

Finally, he backed off and helped me to descend the three steps to the ground.

"Spill." He stood like the Queen's Own Cowboy.

"I think he was in possession of a treasure map. At least when I touched him to check for a pulse, that's the image that came to mind."

Ace frowned. "You practicing necromancy now?"

"Not like I have a choice. It just hit me when I checked to see if he was really deceased." I began to hiccup.

Ace patted my back. "You swallowed too much air. Hold your breath."

The heat of his extra-large hand through my shirt and light fall jacket surprised me, not to mention the jar to my system. The hiccups stopped instantly, but the heat continued.

"I'm fine now." I backed away.

"That you are, Miss McCall. So, a treasure map. Did you find it?"

"Ah, no."

"But you looked, right?"

I didn't trust myself to speak, so I nodded.

"And sprinkled your magical DNA everywhere." He gave another prolonged sigh.

"You wouldn't even know about the map if I hadn't been here. It might be a significant top-pocket find."

"Not if we don't actually have it to hand. Seeing it in your mind is not hard evidence, beautiful."

Aw, beautiful. That was nice to hear. Maybe he was going to let me off lightly after all?

"But at least we have a place to start. You know, maybe I should touch the other guy, see if some residue image remains?" I wanted us to work on this unusual case together. Ace needed my help, more than he knew. I mean, this was my town—I knew pretty much everything that went on…or could find it out. I had a lot of sources, and now apparently, I could add the newly departed to them.

"The other body's already on the way to the medical examiner's office."

"Do you suspect foul play for certain?"

"A second body? And both happen to be drinking hard liquor at the time? You don't think that's pretty significant odds?"

"Apple Pie Moonshine," I corrected him, then could have taped my own mouth shut. *Please don't let that be the cause of death.*

"The famous recipe of your aunt's, right?"

"Stolen by the Hou—Sergei."

"Which explains the awesome rendition of *Battle of the Somme* the last three mornings running by your aunt."

"She was just protecting her own! He pirated her special recipe. She's got a legitimate beef."

"*Had.* And now he's dead. As is Jon Rail."

"No one in town with that last name that I know of. Is he a drifter?"

"You should head home now. I have police work to do." He pulled a pair of blue plastic gloves from his pocket. Where had the department managed to get such an extra-large pair?

"Fine, but for the record, I wasn't trying to hide anything from you. Granny just asked me to check on the camper and I got pulled into things. I really was coming to get you." I explained to make sure he understood I was on his side. But being dismissed didn't sit well and needed addressing as well. "I thought we'd hit a proper quid-pro-quo situation of late, Sheriff."

"I'm always prepared to share what I can. And I appreciate it when you do as well. But I've got a dead body to tend to." I watched him struggle to pull on the gloves.

"Right. Catch you later," I said over my shoulder and headed over to Thor.

On the way back to Skull Cave, I pulled the Jeep to the side of the road to make a quick map of what I'd seen. I've been blessed with a photographic mind, but I wanted to make darn sure I got each and every detail exactly right. As I drew the image on a sketch pad, I began to recognize landmarks. Spirits Springs, Skull Cave and the actual Snowy Lake with tributaries were obvious, as was the highest point within sixty miles, Gold Mountain.

The X was situated on a tributary of Snowy Lake not far from the base of the mountain. One of the hot spots, no doubt, of where the gold had collected eons ago. The area was very rocky and near impossible to navigate, filled with huge granite boulders and dead tree roots and stumps. A lot of local legends said the area was haunted by the unfortunate souls of treasure hunters who had not made it out alive. It wasn't hard to see why. It would be easy to get hurt in that area, and difficult to get help, especially in decades past without helicopter rescue.

I closed the cover of the sketch pad and restarted Thor. Maybe I should wait until dark to investigate? I made a quick U-turn and headed back to the Tea & Tarot, feeling like all I'd been doing today was acting like a pinball. It was past time to hit tilt and squeeze my slippery auntie.

I pushed open the door to the café, only to be greeted by Ivana.

"Charm, my friend." Ivana was alone, enjoying a cup of coffee and looking out through the front window, as if waiting for someone.

"Have you seen Auntie T.J., my very good friend Ivana?" I responded in kind to avoid a meltdown.

"Yes. Gone away."

"Gone where?"

"Your auntie said you go to dance with Big Sheriff? The one where woman asks man?"

"Yes." Where was this headed? *With Ivana, it could be just about anywhere.*

"Maybe we make Hero Sandwich?"

"Sorry. I don't follow."

She waggled her eyebrows, a siren's smile gracing her plush lips playfully outlined with deep red liner and filled in with a matching shiny lipstick. "You know, three sections. You, me and him. Meat sandwich. All go together to dance."

I struggled to keep a straight face. "No, you misunderstand — it's a *couples'* dance. We need another male to make it right. Or female?"

"Female? You swing both ways?" She looked so hot I could see how some women might be tempted, if only she weren't so scary. Was she playing me now? I couldn't tell with Ivana and I wasn't touching her to find out. *No way. I just might learn too much.* And there'd be no coming back from that.

"Aw, no, just one way."

"Fine. You find man for Ivana, and we date twice."

"I think you mean 'double date'."

"Yes. Settled then. What man for Ivana?"

I barely managed not to groan aloud. Now I had to find a date for Ivana *and* keep her from hanging all over Ace at the dance. She really liked my big strong Mountie.

"It's a surprise." What man in his right man would take the chance? Shoot, if only the Hound Dog were still alive. Maybe Bad Billy Bishop? He had a reputation as not worrying overmuch what kind of trouble he stirred up, probably because he'd been a fullback for a professional football until a few years ago. He was a huge man who weighed more than Ace and knew how to take a hit and give 'em too, where it belonged, on the sports field. "When did you see my auntie last?"

"Here. Ivana drink coffee with Auntie."

"Five minutes ago?"

She nodded, languidly holding out five perfectly manicured fire-engine-red fingernails atop an elegant hand as proof.

"Did she say where she was going?"

"Said go home. Play safe."

"That's good." I took a deep breath. *Finally*, something was going right today. But it seemed every bit of information I wormed from Ivana had a steep price tag. Was Bad Billy even free? And more importantly, what could I bribe him with? *Hmm.* He loved chocolate, considering how much he bought made with the sweet ingredient from our café, though that might just be enticement for his many girlfriends. Who knew, maybe he might even meet his match in my Russian boarder?

Snowy Lake was a magical place, built as it was on a crossroads of ley lines and telluric currents. It was cradled in a large valley surrounded by the Gold Mountain on the western side and the Moose Mountains to the east, neither of which was much more than gently rolling hills, but which seemed to attract more than their fair share of otherworldly creatures. And I included myself in that. It was the right place for us. *A great place to hide.* So why did my sister want to leave so badly? Just because I'd come to grips with it didn't mean I totally understood her decision. How was I going to protect her in Hollywood?

Ivana spoke again, interrupting my musing. "Auntie changed mind about Ivana helping with body hide?"

"What are you talking about? What body?" Ivana had my full attention now and I moved closer to her.

"She said you had no time for Auntie—need Ivana. *Tsk-tsk.* Always time to help, my friend. Buy shovel, dig and voila, body gone."

"Right. Well, we'll just see about that. No more hiding the body. The law has already found the body. In fact, two bodies."

"Two. Auntie T.J. has much big ones." She applauded with one raised eyebrow.

"She has a lot of explaining to do is what she has. Thank you, my friend, for being honest with me."

She nodded sagely. "Honesty last resort."

"Too true. Okay, leave my auntie to me. I'll take care of it."

"You bribe?"

I shook my head. "No. No bribing. Just investigating. In fact, I'd best be on my way."

"Buy shovel, just in case."

"No shovel. But a truth serum wouldn't go amiss." I about faced and hurried from the café before I learned something else that would be upsetting. Ivana was a treasure trove of such things.

I jumped into Thor and gunned his motor, backed onto Main Street when it was safe to do so and headed to auntie's house. I was hauling out the big guns this time. *Spill the beans or I'm going straight to your sister, missy.*

Sparkly white salt gleamed in the sunlight—the trail Emma had left led all around the edges of the picturesque cottage. Thoughts of my mother arriving to stay with my auntie brought me up short. How was I going to handle it? The instant roiling in my stomach suggested not well. Maybe I needed a protection spell of my own? My spirit animal was the eagle. It wouldn't hurt to charge a talisman up and wear it for a while. Maybe splurge for a real gold one? The highest level of protection on earth is housed in gold, my personal theory on why ancient aliens might have coveted our planet's resources. According to legend, their depleted atmosphere required the precious stuff to protect them from the sun's damaging rays. Maybe we'd better hold on to all the gold we could, considering the current state of our own atmosphere…

The front door of the gingerbread-style cottage opened abruptly and out stormed Auntie T.J. "What are you doing here, Charm? I thought we agreed that we should lie low for a while?" she hissed, then took my arm and escorted me inside in a bum's rush.

I stumbled and righted myself. "What's the hurry?"

"Prying eyes. Everywhere."

"Have you lost it?" I asked, when the front door was slammed behind us. "What's going on?"

"I've been set up. I need your help."

"After you ran away from me earlier?" I was skeptical. Auntie T.J. ran her own game, in her own time. "I thought you were going to ask for Ivana's?" I couldn't resist.

"Too late for that. The body's been found."

"More like two bodies have been found. I just found a second one in a camper behind the Bowl-a-ram-a. Know anything about that?"

Auntie T.J. went as white as a sheet. "Two. Any moonshine involved?"

"You guessed right. Same MO. What's going on? Are you ready to spill it? Because that's the only way I can help you." I added my own steely-eyed glare for good measure.

"I'll tell you all I know. I was out at Skull Cave loading up my special elixir onto a dolly to haul it to Ladybug to sell at the Homecoming events when Mr. Byrd came to check up on me. He's a very nice man, you know."

I worked hard not to roll my eyes before she continued with her tale. "I had a look-out at the detachment—I'm not senile—which is why I knew it was safe to fill my trunk and get my orders out to everyone. It's Sunday, best day for it. Then we both heard scuffling sounds—you know how sound carries in the caves—then running footsteps. Sylvester went to check and he found Sergei. He suggested I get right out of there, considering that Sergei and I had been in a bit of a standoff lately, making me look guilty, and that he would also take off in another direction. I hightailed it back to town, and well, you know the rest. But Gerald McCleod found the body and reported it before I could get help to hide said body, which meant Sylvester had to stay and confess to finding it as well."

"Why on earth did you not just stay and report it? Not like you did it. What are you not telling me?"

"Nothing."

"Okay, we can confirm everything. Just let me take a reading."

She backed away from me. "No way. I've told you all I know. If that darn McCleod hadn't come along, things would have worked out just fine. Now, you say there's another body. Good grief. What's my sister going to say? She's going to be upset. You got to help me, Charm. Use your coven to add some kind of spell that causes red herrings or something like that. Can you do that?'

"Red herrings? No such thing. All I can do is find out the truth."

"What good is that?" She added a pout that rivaled Star's best. "We need a smokescreen. I'm desperate here. Please, can't you think of something? Chrome won't get you home, you know."

"What does that even mean?" Auntie T.J. was a font of sayings that only had meaning to her. Well, at least they weren't of the cliché variety. I hadn't heard that one before.

A brisk knock on the door made both of us freeze. *Oh shoot.* I just knew who that was with my luck today. Now he was going to think I'd gone behind his back again. And this time, that hadn't been my intention.

Chapter Eight

"Are you going to answer that?" I asked pointedly.

She shook her head and whispered. "Shush. They'll go away."

"Miss Toogood. Are you in there? RCMP. Open up, please."

We both groaned in tandem, recognizing the voice.

"This is *your* fault. If you weren't so involved with that Mountie, he wouldn't be so all up in our business," she hissed.

"My fault! I'm not the one fleeing the scene of a crime."

"He can't know about that. Please, Charm, for your granny's sake, you got to cover for me."

She had me there. But how on earth was I going to keep any of this from Ace? One look at me and he would know I was hiding something big. *Think.* Maybe a spell? Oh goddess, if only I could cast a for-real invisibility spell, I'd even take a side journey to Hades to hide out for the next few minutes if it were possible.

The devil you don't know is sometimes preferable over the one you do.

I snapped my fingers. "I just can't go *abracadabra*, you know. Not to mention it's a waning moon with no punch."

"You must know something that will help. You're the strongest witch from our line since Mary Sarah Toogood crossed the borderlands."

This was the first time anyone had called me a witch, and it set me back on my heels. I mean, we did call ourselves a coven, but it was more in the spirit of friendship and the love of being connected to the goddess, not because we thought of ourselves as witches. *More like super-turbo goddesses.*

Louder knocking resounded, setting the door rocking on its hinges. "I can hear you in there. Open up right now!"

As I speak, shall it be told. As I hear, shall it be told. As I listen, shall it be told. Become the oracle and truth be told. The words flew unbidden into my mind and I nodded once at my auntie. "Let him in. And tell him the danged truth. We're in a safe zone."

"What took you so long?" Ace's expression was somewhat irate. On a scale of one to ten, I'd give it a thirteen and a half.

"Sorry, just plotting strategy. I won. We're going to tell you the truth."

I watched the wind falter in his sails. "Good. Excellent. Well, let's get at it. What can you tell me about your whereabouts this morning, Miss Toogood?"

"Call me Auntie T.J. We're almost related, anyway."

He didn't respond to the poke but waited.

"Tell the truth. Because if you don't, I will."

"Go right ahead, little Miss Smarty Pants."

"My aunt didn't see a ghost carrying a scythe this morning. She was there—"

"Actually, I did. Well, not me per se, but I'm pretty sure baby Ling Ling did. She was scared three times her size right out there on the front street and no one around. No other critter whatsoever." She shook her head so firmly that one of her extra-large hoop earrings went flying over the TV and landed somewhere behind the huge fifty-five-inch screen.

"Oh—" She raised her hand to her empty ear lobe. "I need to find that. I'll look lopsided otherwise. Excuse me a minute. I won't be a sec."

She left Ace and I stranded near the door and rushed across the living room, surprisingly spry for her age, ducking down and out of sight behind the TV set.

"Sorry about that. Auntie's very partial to that pair of earrings."

"Uh-huh. So, in the meantime, tell me what you learned from her before I came."

I quickly filled him in on the few facts I knew. To his credit, he remained stony-faced, not interrupting once until I finished.

"Failure to report a crime is an offense. What was your aunt thinking?"

We both watched my auntie finally appear from behind the set like a Jill-in-the-box, clutching the five-inch gold hoop in her hand. "Here we go. Just need to dust it off and we'll be all set. Would you like some tea, coffee, cocoa, a beer, whiskey, brandy...? Hmm, maybe I have some lemon gin? What will it be, Constable?"

"I'm fine. Now, before you take care of your jewelry concerns, if you would be so kind as to share—"

But it was too late. My auntie had swept out of the room.

A tic began under Ace's right eye. I pretended to grimace. "Sorry. She's a bit of a stickler for appearances. Feels off balance, I would guess, with only one earring on."

"I would imagine." His droll tone made me grimace for real.

"She's just nervous, Ace. She's not normally like this."

He licked his lips, drawing my full attention.

"Are you certain you're not thirsty?" I asked, unable to look away from their fine plushness. Everything about Ace was so darn fine. From the top of his awesome Stetson to the bottom of his regulation boots, he was a prime male specimen. I sighed, feeling thirsty myself. What was I going to do about this unwanted attraction? I was getting dangerously close to just throwing myself at him willy-nilly.

He caught me watching him. Our eyes met and locked. A spark lit in the depths of his and neither of us looked away. Did my eyes also spark when he looked into them?

His hand came up and he touched my cheek with the back of his fingers. He murmured while he stroked my skin ever so gently. "Peaches and cream. Absolute perfection."

I swallowed. "Th-thank you."

I was about to reach up and touch his skin when my auntie flounced into the room again, making me wince from all the cackling she had going on. "Good thing I'm here as chaperone, eh?"

She stopped in front of Ace. "Okay, I'm all yours, Mr. Mountie. Ask away."

"Why were you out at Skull Cave this morning?"

"Sorry, can't say."

I groaned, shaking my head. "Tell him what you were doing there or so help me goddess —"

"Then you need to leave so I can talk to him alone. I won't say anything else in front of my niece." She wouldn't look me in the eye as she spoke, gazing off with incredible interest at the living room drapes.

Her words stunned me to the core. I had nothing. No words issued from my mouth.

"Charm, if you wouldn't mind, I would like a few minutes alone with your aunt?"

"Fine. I'll leave." Now it was my turn to flounce off. Were my feelings hurt? On a scale of one to ten, it was a home run.

Driving Thor back down the street, I reviewed the facts. My auntie was involved in this thing right up to her chin, though she'd most likely only been at the scene of the murder due to her meeting up with Tweedy Byrd at the cave. I'd bet she was now busy swearing Ace to secrecy over the unsavory reason she had been there.

I shook my head, still hurt that she couldn't just come right out with it. What connected the two deaths? *Find the connection, find the murderer.* Where was I going to find a lead? More information was definitely in order. *Eureka.* Yes, that was it! I needed to puzzle out Sergei's ledger. I'd guess the answer to the mystery existed in those pages. It was rumored he kept it out at Skull Cave, hidden from prying eyes. And one final fact — I was starving.

I parked in back of the café this time and slipped into the kitchen, ready to chase down my prey, muffins or scones or most anything not nailed down. To my happy surprise, coven members were busy at all the counters, mixing and pouring batter into cake pans.

"Charm, there you are!" Emma rushed over to greet me, flour on both cheeks and something that looked and smelled like vanilla splashed on her apron. "We'd thought we'd give you a hand what with everything that's going on. How's your auntie? What's the latest?"

"Thanks for all this." I waved my hands around, taking in all the smiling helpers. "I found another body."

Her eyes sprang wide open. "No. Where? How awful for you."

"In a camper behind the Bowl-a-ram-a. A man called Jon Rail." I didn't add the details of what I had learned because I didn't want to explain how I had gotten them. It still kind of spooked me, no pun intended.

"Jon Rail?" Christine turned from placing a cake pan in the convection oven. "Sean mentioned something about meeting him."

"When?"

"Bowling night. A bunch of his friends went there on Saturday to play a few games."

"So, he was still fine yesterday. How did Sean come to meet him?"

"I'm not sure. Sean just said he seemed friendly enough, and that when Sean asked if he was there to celebrate Homecoming, the man acted a bit strange, saying it was going to be a Homecoming all right, in kind of an ominous way. Then Sergei came over with Floyd Millhouse and Eric Taylor, and the men all went out together. Sean said they seemed friendly enough."

"Hmm, Floyd of the odd aura." I remembered Tulip's words from earlier.

"And now that guy's dead too?" Christine looked upset. "How is this even possible? Two dead men in our town in one day? Snowy Lake's not like this. Do you think we're safe? Maybe we all need a protection charm?"

I rushed to reassure her. "I'll make you up something right away. Don't worry. I'm sure we'll discover that the deaths are connected for good reason."

"There's no good reason for someone to die before their time." Christine looked less than convinced.

I grabbed a muffin from the display and began to munch. I had too much to do to spend much time devoted to eating, but my stomach was screaming blue bloody murder.

"Did moonshine factor into the second death as well?" Tulip asked, sparing me a glance. She had finished icing a large slab of cake and had handed it off to Star for the final flourishes. Star had a well-deserved reputation for fancying up just about anything, and she was particularly adept at cake decorating.

"Yeah, unfortunately. A mason jar of the stuff was spilled all over his camper." I shuddered at the memory of finding the body and connecting with him in such a strange way. Why had I been shown the treasure map? *Not like I want to go treasure hunting.* At least not in the badlands, where the gold was supposedly hidden.

"Did you learn anything else?" Tulip asked, always the sharp one. "Your aura's gone all kerflooey."

I chewed on my bottom lip. "A few things. Nothing I'm prepared to share at the moment."

"How are we going to help if you aren't honest?" Star asked.

"Okay, I saw a few things. The guy was here looking for treasure, I think."

"Probably heard about the recent finds by the Altima Exploration company," Tulip said with a sage nod of her head.

"Maybe." I ignored all the speculative looks of the women when the name of the gold company was brought up. She-who-shall-not-be-mentioned was one of the company's geologists, connected through the University of Manitoba graduate program. An old family friend of Ace's. *Yeah, right!* More like an old family snake-in-the-grass. All up in Ace's business and using a perfectly nice boyfriend of hers to garner my man's full attention by strategically breaking up with said boyfriend to garner sympathy. I mean, who does that? She really deserved to be poppet trounced by my crew, even though I didn't encourage such things. I mean, if I were a witch, I was a good magic one. Or at least I tried to be.

"What specifically did you learn?" Tulip asked pointedly.

"That our auntie is up to her old tricks." Then I felt bad for the decoy lob. I shouldn't be sharing old family skeletons with everyone and bringing it so close to granny.

"What do you mean?" Tulip came closer and stood right in front of me. I swallowed the last of the apple-cinnamon muffin and took a swig of water from a bottle I grabbed off the counter before answering.

"Sorry. I shouldn't have mentioned that. But, yes, I learned about a specific treasure map when I touched the dead guy." I had no choice but to throw it out there to avoid anymore discussion of auntie's antics.

"You mean like necromancy?" Emma asked, her eyes rounding into the familiar owl-shape.

"Yeah, something like that."

"That's awesome," Tulip said, the first one onboard. "Oh *wow*, I can't wait to share with my followers. It's just so perfect."

"Figures," Star grumbled. "You guys get all the best stuff."

"No, *absolutely* not. I don't want this getting around. I'm calling a Warrior-Maiden."

Everyone groaned. *Perfect.* I had just put a tighter lid on things that the Federal Government ever could on a UFO event. If they discussed it now, they were in peril for being hauled up in front of the coven for spilling a goddess secret of secrets.

"So, what do we call it when we have to discuss it with you? In private, of course," Tulip, ever-the-practical, asked.

"Call it an angel, as in, what did that 'angel' have to say?" It sounded so much better than *dead guy talking*. All kidding aside, euphemisms helped me get through the day. The famous McCall realistic streak was also pushing me to not focus on the fact two persons were dead but on what could be done about finding justice for them.

"Now, can we get down to even more serious business?"

"What?" Tulip asked.

"Making great cakes," I said with a grin, joining the conga line of awesome bakers.

Chapter Nine

With the freezer now filled with delectable cakes worthy of a royal fest and the final coven member given a fully charged protective sigil or amulet, I prepared for the night's planned exploits – Operation Get Ledger.

I raced upstairs to my bedroom, crept by Ivana's apartment as stealthy as a ninja in a martial arts movie and hurried inside my own suite, quietly closing the door on its newly oiled hinges. *Why wake a sleeping tigress?* Changing into head-to-toe black, I added a warm windbreaker over my turtleneck and a stocking cap to cover my hair, even though it was raven black.

I tucked the new eagle amulet inside my clothing. The warmth of the gold warmed my fingers, little sparkles of electricity adding their own zing. Maybe I should add camouflage makeup to my paler-than-pale skin? *Better not.* It'd be hard to explain if a snoopy Mountie was watching and stopped me on some trumped-up charge. Or, more likely, just to talk. Though our 'talks' were getting hotter by the day...

Okay, back to the matter at hand. Though it was almost three kilometers to Skull Cave from town, I would be hoofing it across country to avoid detection. I slipped the homemade pepper spray and sturdy flashlight equipped with fresh batteries into my jacket pocket, then donned black gloves. Next, I exited my small, cozy apartment still decorated in Star's favorite colors of midnight blue and gold. I had let her at the place when I first moved in, and it had made her so happy.

One of these days I needed to find my own style. Even Ace had mentioned the place wasn't quite how he saw me. What was my style? *Probably on the lighter side. Creams and whites would be nice. Make the space airier.* I had a lot of time to think of all this as I crept by Ivana's apartment one tiny, tiny baby step at a time. I'd swear she has bat hearing, and the last thing I wanted was to draw attention to my nocturnal comings and goings.

I made it safely back down to the kitchen. Leaving the lights off to avoid detection, I slipped out through the back door, remembering to lock it behind me. If not, Ace would check on his rounds and wake up the whole town if I didn't answer his call. I shook my head. *What a protective man.* It was as if he didn't get that I was safer than most, what with the blessed goddess gifts I had been endowed with, plus the spells I had learned.

Jogging down the alley behind the Tea & Tarot, I kept a sharp eye out for any pedestrians. I didn't want to be stopped by friends or neighbors and have to explain myself. I managed a fairly decent clip and made Skull Cave in under an hour. Now for the hard part. Even though I was over most of my claustrophobia for confined spaces, caused by being locked in dark cupboards for hours on end when we were children, I couldn't be certain it would not rear its ugly head again. The memory took me to a place I was refusing to think about right now. *My mother.*

Taking a deep breath, I pulled out my flashlight and switched it on. *Here goes nothing.* Touching the golden eagle amulet through my clothing, I headed inside the yawing mouth of the cave, fear riding me every step of the way. What if that darn ghost was still roaming around? Which reminded me, I need to have a discussion with baby Ling Ling and find out if she knew who the ghost belonged to. *Carrying a scythe, indeed.* But what if that fact was actually true? The image spooked me and sweat began to trickle even faster between my shoulder blades and under my arm pits, my scalp itching under the knit cap.

Navigating the narrow alleys of the huge Skull Cave underground abyss was challenging at the best of times, the experience not enhanced by a too-rapid beating heart and a mind known for its imaginative qualities. *Serenity now* pronouncements every few steps didn't cut it.

When I made the small alcove where the body of Sergei had been found, I breathed a sigh of relief.

I slipped under the yellow police tape and headed for the rock face. *Please, please, let no one else have found the hidden vault.* The wall appeared sound, with no rocks pulled out. *Good.* I slipped my fingers into the cracks of the removable rock near the bottom of the wall, tugging out the cover. I knew about Sergei's hiding spot, having spent a bit of time in his mind before he'd passed, when I'd bumped into him on the sidewalk. I wasn't a big collector of secrets, unless someone was thinking of something when I touched them, then the knowledge passed into me.

But sometimes, it's sweet...like now. I pulled out his black book with satisfaction. Now, maybe I could find out something that would help, like who he'd seen today. One thing he was good at other than stealing formulas — keeping meticulous records.

I opened his ledger and checked the last entries, running my forefinger down the list. *Yes.* Five separate lines for each person who had bought moonshine today. Five names to add to my memory bank. Footfalls suddenly resounded down the tunnel and about gave me a freakin' heart attack. I shoved the book back into the pick-axe-hewn hidey-hole and pushed the covering rock back into place with both hands.

Turn off the flashlight or not? One thing instantly came to mind, that it was best to be found on the *other* side of the RCMP crime tape. Hurrying to exit the alcove, I checked my mental map of the entire Skull Cave structure, trying to locate other spots I could hide in close by. *Hmm.* Just fifteen feet away was a side tunnel that led to a seldom-used part of the system. For good reason — it dropped off into a sheer cliff and into a deep pool of ice-cold water that had no bottom. Well, one not yet discovered. I ducked under the warning sign, hurried to the tunnel and waited as quietly as I could, my heart beating like a jackrabbit's.

The footsteps came ever closer and I pushed up against the creepy cave wall, turning off my flashlight. The steps went right on by, so unfortunately, I could neither see anyone nor even catch a glimpse of movement in the darkness. I waited for as long as I could, then quietly ventured back the way I'd come, using the walls as my guide. When I thought it safe to do so, I turned the flashlight back on. Maybe I should have taken the darn ledger outright? Was there even more incriminating evidence hidden inside its black cover? I was no thief. I would have returned it. I just hadn't wanted to be caught with it in my possession in case I was searched. Imagining Ace doing the searching wasn't helping my perspiration situation one bit.

I began the long cross-country jog back to town. There was no vehicle in the lot where visitors would normally have parked to enter either Spirit Springs or Skull Cave. Had they also come on foot? That surprised me and I felt vulnerable, like someone was on my tail all the way back to the café. I was never so happy to unlock the back door to the kitchen and get safely inside.

Okay. I set my key down on the counter and reviewed the list of suspects, transferring their names to a sheet of paper. Tor and Kate Johnson, Josie Davidson, Floyd Millhouse and Eric Taylor.

Hmm. Tor Johnson's wife, Kate, had recently had an affair with Sergei before he'd taken up with Josie Davidson. *Talk about a volatile threesome with plenty of crisscross there for problems.* Eric was a moonshine man himself, so the competition factor came into play, and he had been seen with the victim earlier. Floyd bought the illegal product to sell to his guests at the Lakeside Inn on the sly. He'd more likely want to keep Sergei alive than not. The pirated recipe had to be popular with guests and the bottom line.

I drummed my fingers on the counter, contemplating the suspects and making an action plan for the morning. I would need to interview all the moonshine partakers and find out what they knew. That was, if I could get them to thinking about what I needed to know when I touched them. Josie Davidson would be the easiest. I'd get to her first, her being a regular visitor to our café and often getting one of us to do a reading.

Yawning, I caught Ling Ling watching me.

"Yes, I need to find out what you know as well, baby. Whose ghost did you run into this morning?"

She gave me the thousand-mile-stare that cats are known for when they feel slighted.

"Sorry I ran out of time to get to the bottom of it this morning." I sighed. "It was such a busy time and there was so much to do to protect the family. You understand, right? You work at protecting our family as well. What can I do to make it up to you? A special treat? Some fresh fried fish tomorrow?"

She eyed me a few seconds longer then moved in her most queenly manner across the black-and-white linoleum to my side, rubbing against my calf, her signal that all was forgiven.

"Thank you, baby Ling Ling. You're the best, sweetest, smartest cat in the whole universe." I stretched my spine. "I think this has been the longest day ever. If this is only Sunday, what's this week going to bring?"

"*Meow.*"

"Yeah, you're right, it doesn't bode well. But now I know who to target for my investigation, so that's something at least. Oh, and yeah, I discovered a new gift today. One you might appreciate. I can get a reading off a dead body."

"*Meow, meow.*"

"Yeah, better to see ghosts. But I'll take any extra help I can get. Right?"

"*Meow, meow, meow.*"

"Yup, time for bed."

The pair of us crept up the staircase and past Ivana's door, being careful not to converse until we were inside my apartment.

Too tired to shower, I left my clothes where they fell, brushed my teeth and climbed into bed while Ling Ling curled up on the opposite pillow. She's a definite Princess-and-the-pea-type. One little lump and she can't settle.

"Please go to sleep. We'll talk in the morning." I was way too tired to go through the alphabet with her to discover the name of the elusive ghost.

"*Meow.*"

Drifting off to the sounds of her ceaseless snoring, I wondered if one of those no-snoring aids they sold at the drugstore might be of assistance to my furry baby? I made a mental note to look into it.

I must have fallen asleep, because the next thing I knew sunlight was streaming in my bedroom windows, announcing a new day. Monday beckoned with a rush of good energy to get to the bottom of things. *My town, my chance to help. I mean, I've read every Agatha Christie book ever written.* Armed with all that expert sleuthing and deductive information, I could figure out a Snowy Lake murder investigation quicker than anyone, especially with Ace on my side.

I hopped out of bed, having no doubt of my drive to solve the mystery. Now I just needed a bit of good luck, help from my fellow goddesses, and things would be wrapped up in a jiff…

Chapter Ten

Having turned on the coffee maker and the essential air vent above the stove, I slipped some fresh perch from the refrigerator and placed a nice chunk in a cast iron frying pan dedicated to the delicacy. *Ling Ling's favorite breakfast.* She was not in evidence this morning yet, but the fragrance of frying fish would have her rounded up in no time.

A loud knocking on the kitchen door startled me, and I dropped my spoon onto the table with a clatter. I glanced at the clock. Six a.m. was a little early for visitors. Even Ace, who checked in nearly every morning, usually waited until seven o'clock.

I checked through the peephole that Ace had insisted on and observed Kate Johnson standing there and looking anxiously around, her face cast in shadows in the pre-dawn light.

Opening the door, I beckoned her inside, not bothering to hide my surprise. "Morning, Kate."

"Hey, Charm. Sorry to bother you so early, but I saw your light on and I needed to see you." She looked even more nervous close up, shivering in her coat, her light brown hair yanked up into a haphazard ponytail. Kate works as a dental hygienist and is good at her job, calm and professional on a daily basis. This morning that persona seemed to have left the station.

"Coffee?"

"Please. I missed my usual caffeine fix in my rush to get out of the house this morning." Kate took the steaming cup from my hands and gave me a grateful smile. "Thanks."

"Sit and tell me what I can do for you?" The fact that Kate was on my suspect list was immensely satisfying, because she looked ready to share something of importance. And since everyone in town and their dog or cat knew of my gifts, it didn't take a rocket scientist to pick up on that she wasn't here at this time of day for idle chit-chat.

She perched on a chair and held the cup warming her hands, her pale face gaining a bit of color as she sipped the heady brew. She sniffed the air. "Is that fish frying?"

"Right." I jumped up and checked the frying pan. Grabbing a spatula, I lifted the fish from the pan to let it cool on the counter until her highness made her appearance.

I sat and faced Kate. "Okay, all set now."

She quirked her lips upward in a look that was more grimace than smile, then ran her forefinger over the rim of her coffee cup. "Do you believe in ghosts?"

Her question caught me off guard. "I think some souls have more trouble than others moving on to the next world. Why? What's up? Do you want me to do a reading for you? Have you lost something?"

She pursed her lips, obviously thinking. I took a sip of my coffee and waited. The rooster clock ticked over my head, reminding me of a heartbeat with its soothing, rhythmic energy. No wonder people soothed puppies by tucking a clock into their bed at night.

"Is it about what happened in our town yesterday? Two deaths in one day." I sighed in dismay, trying to prompt her. Was she troubled about Sergei? Maybe she also knew Jon Rail?

"Terrible is right." She shook her head, her ponytail swinging from side to side. "I don't know if you knew, but Sergei and I dated for a while in high school."

I remained silent, just nodding, not wanting to interrupt the flow of words, though her imploring look saddened me.

"We've remained friends, something that Tor doesn't understand."

"Hmm."

She pressed her lips together. "Sergei came to me last night, after midnight."

I startled and sat up straighter. "His spirit came to you?" We both knew he'd been dead for hours by then.

"Yes." She shuddered visibly, her throat rippling as she swallowed. "I was in the bath and he appeared nearby."

"Did he stay long? Say anything?"

"He drew with his finger in the steamy mirror — I like a hot bath in a closed room — then vanished."

"What did the words say?"

"No words, something that looked like a drawing, maybe a map. It was all squiggles and other stuff."

"A map? Hold on." I jumped up and retrieved my sketchpad from the counter, opened it to my drawing from yesterday then plunked it down in front of her. "Any resemblance to this?"

She squinted at the lines. "Kind of. The wavy river lines and Gold Mountain looks about right. Also, there was an X just like that near the base. Yeah, this is pretty close. How did you come by this? Did Sergei visit you too?" She looked awestruck, hanging on to my every word.

"No. I found the body of Jon Rail." I hesitated. I knew it was possible I was talking to the murderess. I couldn't forget that, however remote it seemed at the moment.

"Did he have a map? Do you think the map had something to do with Sergei's death? Do you think that's what he was trying to tell me?"

"Would you mind if I touched you, took a reading? Asked some questions?" If she were the murderer — and I was more than certain now that he had been murdered, with two men dying in similar situations — it wouldn't be likely she'd let me. I gotten a reputation these past few months for being able to help solve investigations with my hands-on-readings.

"Sure. Anything that will assist finding out what happened to poor Sergei."

I took her outstretched hands into mine. "Just close your eyes and think about the event with the ghost first. Okay?"

She nodded and we both closed our eyes. I was instantly teleported to the yellow-and-white bathroom in her home, seeing the décor from the vantage point of the bathtub through Kate's eyes. A glass tumbler sat on the edge of the tub to my right, I felt the trickle of alcohol in my bloodstream and the warmth of the hot, bubbly bathwater seeping into my naked body in a wonderfully soothing way.

Then a spirit began to emerge out of thin air, its outline appearing to be male. It began to look like Sergei, and I sat up straighter, nearly knocking over the drinking glass from the shock of recognizing him. A ghostly finger rose and began to draw on the foggy mirror, a map resembling the one I had just shared with Kate.

The image faded. "Did you see him?" Kate asked.

"Yes. Please, show me what happened when you went to see him earlier in the day."

She yanked her hands away and I opened my eyes to see her glaring at me. "How did you know about that?"

"Do you have something to hide? Were you just buying moonshine, or did something else happen?" I pressed. "I can eliminate you as a possible suspect if you show me what happened."

She looked torn.

"Please, Kate. It will help with the investigation. I don't care that the two of you were more than good friends. It's none of my concern. I just want to see that Sergei and Jon get proper justice for what happened to them."

"Maybe it was your Auntie T.J.'s moonshine that killed the pair of them?"

"What? You know that's not what happened. I can't help you if you don't show me." I tried not to take offense at her words.

"Yeah, I know. But I had nothing to do with what happened to either of them." She shook her head.

"Then show me."

Still she hesitated. Then a meow behind me alerted me to Ling Ling arriving through her convenient cat door.

I got up and retrieved the piece of fish, setting it on a pristine china plate in front of our fluffy white and apricot-colored feline.

"*Meow.*" She bestowed her blessing and set about having her breakfast in that fastidious manner unique to cats.

"She's beautiful," Kate said.

"And a bit too smart for her own good." Baby Ling Ling ignored me and continued with her feast.

I sat back down and took Katie's hands again. "Please, let's finish the reading before someone else interrupts."

"Okay."

Though obvious reluctance lined her tone, I held on to her hands firmly and closed my eyes. "Show me the time you spent with him in Skull Cave."

A few seconds later I found myself walking down the path to the entranceway then ducking inside, moving rapidly toward the alcove where Sergei dispensed his moonshine to his regulars. He looked surprised to see me, his forehead furrowing into a straight line. He looked furtively around as if he expected someone to jump out at him from the shadows at any second. I assured him I was alone, and he looked a bit more relaxed before he gestured at his stock of different-sized jugs, asking me if I wanted some. I nodded and he handed me a four-litre container of the Apple Pie Moonshine with a smirk. I handed him some bills that he waved aside, saying it was on the house. He made some notations in his little black ledger and I asked him not to. I didn't want Tor to know I had visited him today. He said not to worry and pointed out the hidey hole for the book.

A brisk knock on the door startled us and with our hands no longer connected, the scene faded. "You like moonshine?" I asked.

She blushed. "Yeah, I've been drinking more than I should, I know. Things haven't been that great at home." She meant her affair with Sergei had added tension. *No kidding, Einstein.*

She continued with a shrug of her narrow shoulders. I was fairly certain now she'd had little to do with Sergei's demise. I had experienced no rage or sense of her up to something when she had met with him, just an intense craving for alcohol. "And I really like the taste of apple pie. I also buy from your auntie." She sounded defensive and I smiled to reassure her.

"I'd better get the door." I jumped up and hurried to answer. Ace's handsome mug greeted me this time.

"Morning, darlin'." He glanced around me, spying Kate. "Company so early."

"Morning, Constable." Kate got up from the table and rinsed her cup hurriedly at the sink. "I should be going. Thanks for the coffee, Charm."

"Anytime."

She slipped out past Ace, her smile a little forced.

"What was that all about?"

"Seems everyone's been seeing ghosts."

His eyebrows vanished under the rim of his awesome Stetson. "Whose ghost?"

Ling Ling looked over at me as well from her vantage point of the top of her climbing cat tree, her pretty blue eyes suggesting interest in my response.

"Apparently Sergei's. Was that the same ghost as you saw yesterday, baby?"

She didn't meow, so no, it wasn't. I'd need to play her game fully to find out. *Later*, I promised.

"Want some coffee?"

"Please." He took off his hat and hung it from a hook near the table we sat at now most mornings, taking the seat Kate had just vacated. I filled a mug with the steaming rich brew and plunked it down in front of him. He took it black, making it easy. Most things about Ace were easy, now that we knew each other a bit better. Still, on some days, if we weren't careful, sparks flew. *Even real ones.* I was thinking of yesterday's lamplight fiasco.

"So, any news?" I asked, joining him at the table.

"Looks like you might be party to some yourself this morning. Pretty early for a visitor." He took a sip of coffee and pinned me in place with those rich brown eyes of his that never failed to send my body into a tailspin.

"Kate was needing to unburden herself. I'm a good listener."

"Was it about the trouble with her husband?"

So, he knew about the affair. It was a strong motive for murder.

"Yeah, but I don't think she had anything to do with it. She just wanted some—" I stopped myself in the nick of time, not wanting to tattletale on another over an illegal activity.

"Moonshine. It's okay. I'm not going to arrest her for that offense. Right now, we've got bigger fish to fry, if you'll excuse the cliché."

"Do we know what killed them?" I suspected it had to have been an ingested poison.

"Not yet. The medical examiner's still doing the autopsies."

A sudden thought arose and scared me into speaking without thinking. "What if the moonshine is poisoned? Oh, my goodness, we'd better warn everyone who bought some yesterday!"

"Other than a general announcement over a bullhorn, how are we going to do that? We'd need a list of people who visited Sergei yesterday so we could warn them, and nothing found so far gives us any indication he kept meticulous records of every sale. Not like he needed them for tax purposes."

I gave a guilty start and got up for another cup of coffee to cover it. Didn't work. He was all over it like white on rice.

"Okay, spill."

"What? You reading my mind now?" I accused him as I poured a cup, leaving room for sugar and cream.

This time Ace looked a bit guilty for a nanosecond and my heart about dropped in my shoes when I caught the fleeting micro-expression. It was gone so fast that I wondered if I had imagined it.

"I thought you wanted us to be a team? What did you find out—you come across a ledger or list or anything?" He narrowed his eyes at me.

"We are on the same team! Sergei kept a ledger. Out at Skull Cave."

"You're just mentioning this now?" Thunderclouds rolled across his handsome face, threatening hail.

"I didn't think to mention it yesterday. It was such a crazy day. It's behind a rock. I could show you if that would help?"

He got to his feet and picked up his hat with deliberate actions as if he were trying to restrain himself before setting it in place. "Lead the way."

Chapter Eleven

"Now? You want to go out to Skull Cave right this moment?" I looked around my cozy kitchen. Baby Ling Ling gave me a look that suggested I had earned another trip to the scary cave system for my temporary lapse in judgment.

"Yes, *now*. We have people to warn. You want to be responsible for not taking care of warning them of the danger?" He looked scandalized, as though I were one nickel shy of a loonie.

Guilt sent me into an even bigger tailspin. "I already know who needs to be warned. I can take care of it right now. Least I can do." Freakin' A, Kate was one of them!

"What?"

I thought he might be counting to ten, so I rushed to use the kitchen phone, which was our one phone connected to a landline. It was the only way to guarantee service in this part of the world.

Kate answered on the second ring, making me breathe easier. I kept my back to Ace to avoid another pointed shot. "Kate, it's Charm." I didn't give her any time to answer but rushed ahead to ask, "Did you drink any of the moonshine you got yesterday from Sergei?"

"Yes, it was good stuff. Drank a few glasses while I had my bath last night. You know, when the ghost appeared."

"Okay. And it tasted fine? No aftereffects?'

"No. I feel great actually. Talking with you made be feel better. You're a good listener. Should I be worried?"

"Just a sec." I put my hand over the phone. "Kate drank a few glasses last night and says she feels fine still, and she did look well when I saw her earlier. When I gave her a reading, her body felt one hundred percent healthy, other than her craving for alcohol." *Hmm. Maybe I can help her with that?*

"Okay, that's good. Unless it's a slow-acting poison? We need to know what it was right now." He was in pure police mode now. "Okay, I'll call the medical examiner, and you call the others on the list. You do have a list, right?"

I nodded, guilty as Hades.

Ten minutes later and I had warned everyone on my suspect list *not* to drink the recently purchased product. Other than Kate, no one else had drunk any yet, so I felt a bit better. Too much had happened yesterday — the worry for Auntie T.J., finding the body and gaining a strange new gift — that maybe I might be forgiven for not thinking of the possibility? I prayed it was so.

"Before you say anything, I'm sorry. I didn't think about that possibility. Do you think that was a fresh batch? What if someone bought some we don't know about and is about to drink it?" Horror overcame me and I slumped down onto the kitchen chair, my legs turning to rubber.

Ace took pity on me. He came over and rubbed my back, instantly making me feel better. "Let's go get the ledger. We can figure this out. With our two brains working in tandem, we're a heck of a team. Your nickname's not Brainiac for nothing, you know. Everyone slips up. Me included."

Our relationship took a deeper turn at that moment. His quick understanding and forgiveness meant a lot. I swallowed my worry. Yes, we could right this thing. Surely there was a code for which batch he had been selling? Then we could know how many people had bought the suspect moonshine and who else to warn, if any.

"I slipped up. I'm sorry, Ace. Thanks." I hesitated before continuing. "You're right, we can fix this thing. Alert any others who may have bought the product. Okay, let's go and do this thing." I grabbed a coat hanging by the back door and we exited the café.

I hopped into Ace's SUV and buckled myself in.

"Okay, new rules from now on. We share what we know as soon as possible—at least, the parts my job allows me to tell you. But there's nothing to stop you from sharing everything ASAP, right?"

I was about to protest, saying he should be sharing everything with me too, when I stopped myself, tamping down my instant ire at being left out of any part of a loop. After all, I do have the help of a lot of magic to keep me onstream for those things he couldn't share.

"Okay. I'll share what I know with you right away. Does that work for you, Constable?"

"Perfectly." He could be so adorable when he was getting his way. Of course, it usually was for everyone else's own good as well.

He drove us down the alleyway headed out of town, turning onto the logging road a couple of minutes later. The trip was far shorter than my midnight jog, and with the sun now peeking over the edge of the world, a fine moment to be out and about.

Ace appeared deep in thought and I hesitated to interrupt. Solving crimes took a great deal of concentration and dedication, studying a problem from every logical angle.

In the parking lot near Spirit Springs, he shut off the vehicle. We both jumped out and headed for Skull Cave. The birds were just beginning their morning song. Spray from the hot springs hit the colder air and turned it to sparkling crystals, holding all the colors of the universe in their many-sided prisms. It was my favorite time of day to take a walk, and today was no different.

"What did the coroner say?" I asked.

"Nothing definite yet, but he suspects poison, of course. He was working on testing when I called. He'll call back soon as he knows."

"Good. I hope we can find a batch number in the ledger. Fingers crossed that those he sold to yesterday were the only people at risk." I kept a sharp look out for black bears. Soon they would be hibernating, but not today. At least Ace carried a gun. I had forgotten my pepper spray in the rush.

At the cave entrance, he turned to me. "How are you doing with your claustrophobia?" Ace had rescued me, carried me right out of Skull Cave in his very capable arms a couple of months back when I had entered it for a good reason, so he had the right to ask.

"Better. Last night I had no problem whatsoever." Then I groaned. TMI, no doubt.

He blinked at me. My safety-first kind of guy let the information sink in while I picked at the scant polish left on one of my fingernails.

"What time was this?" His words sent cold water down my spine.

"Not that late. I just wanted to check on the ledger. You know, make sure it was still there."

"Did you take it?" A second shiver.

"No! Of course not!" Then I remembered how I had taken Mrs. Hurst's bank statements during our first investigation. I hoped he had forgotten. I mean, that had been months ago. I'd matured since then.

"Good. That's something at least."

We entered the cave's mouth together, the chill instantly noticeable.

"I heard some rumors…"

"Yeah, what about?" Curious, I glanced over at him, but the dimness kept me from observing him as well as I would have liked.

"That for the Sadie Hawkins dance, the women bring some kind of small bag that they give to their partner. A hint or nudge at what they want from them? Any truth to that?"

"Ah—yeah." I realized I hadn't made my own Promise Bag yet. A coy smile came over me that I hid from him. This could be fun with a capital F.U.N.

"Interesting. Ah, we're here." He stopped in front of the police tape.

"It's over here." We both ducked under the yellow streamer and I pointed to the spot. "Right there."

Ace moved closer and laid his hands on the wall, tugging out the stone with less trouble than I had last night. He pulled out the ledger. Holding it in one hand, he reached for his flashlight, shining it on the page.

"You left the page intact," he said.

"Well, it was the right thing to do. I just remembered the list is all."

"Useful thing, photographic memory."

"So, what else can we learn?" I nudged in closer to his nice warm body in an effort to see, finding it more of a distraction. I pressed my lips together and made myself concentrate on the figures. His lemony soap and sandalwood aftershave tickled my senses, and I took a breath of appreciation. *Such a nice, clean, sexy fragrance.* I breathed in deeper still. Yes, just a hint of manly musk underneath. *Oh. My. Goddess.*

He pointed at the page, jerking me away from my daydream. "He's coded everything. This is the third Apple Pie recipe he's used. And he just began selling that batch yesterday. See, APB3C1. Apple Pie, Batch 3, Customer 1. Number 5 was Floyd Millhouse, the last person he sold to. He bought the most too. Twenty-five liters."

"Well, he does have a bigger client base at the motel."

"Okay, that goes well beyond drinking a bit of homebrew, if he's distributing moonshine to that extent. I will be dealing with him today." The steel in his voice convinced me of his intentions.

"So, that means everyone's safe for the moment." The thought took a bit of the edge off my guilt.

"Two people dead. I don't want you getting complacent, Miss McCall. Until we get to the bottom of this thing, everyone's a suspect. So far, with no obvious motive, the situation is fluid. Always. Stay. Alert."

"Goes without sayin', Constable."

He gave me a look that made me want to roll my eyes. "I should be getting back to get ready to open for business soon."

"Yes. I need to get going as well."

He held the yellow RCMP crime-scene tape up a bit for me and we both exited the alcove. "I want to make myself very clear. No more hiding things from me, even if they don't seem important at the time. Obstructing police business is nothing to be proud of. Now. How did you know about the ledger?"

I bit my tongue to keep from stepping in it again, concentrating on the question. "It was a fortuitous accident. I bumped into him on the sidewalk a few months ago and got a good image of him hiding the ledger in the cave."

"Lots of people believe everything happens for a reason. I've been reading an autobiography of an emergency room physician on how even doctors have experienced moments of sudden intuition that didn't always make logical sense at the time, but then it helped save a patient's life. There is order to the universe." He punctuated his remarks with a nod.

"Granny's always saying that. That you learn what you need ahead of time, if you but pay attention." Ace and I were the perfect fit on the intellectual level, both loving to learn new things. However, we were also excellent at bumping heads. Well, it was nice to be great at things anyway.

We'd reached the cave's entrance and I stepped out into the sunshine, a good man by my side. Taking a moment to turn my face up toward its healing warmth, I offered a quick word of thanks for the sun. Ancient peoples knew of its importance. *Yes, simple pleasurers are the best.*

"I heard that your mother is expected back in town soon. How are you doing with that? I know you've had your issues with her."

"Issues! That's putting it mildly." I rubbed at my forehead. I felt ill-equipped to deal with her right now. Why couldn't she just stay away?

"Okay." He nodded, his expression troubled.

"I'm sorry. It's just talk of her always puts me in a dark place." *Like she did to us as children.* But at least I was getting over the condition. I'd been into the dim cave twice in twenty-four hours, and each time it was getting easier. Or maybe it was due to the strong, stalwart Mountie at my side? Constable Ace Collins was the type to take a bullet for another. I could read it in every cell in his awesome, very, very fit body.

"Well, if you ever need to talk about it, I'm here for you. Always. I want you to know that. At least according to all the books I've been reading."

I swallowed over the instant lump that tightened my throat. "You've been reading about this stuff?"

"Of course. It affects you, Charm. I want to be able to help you."

"That's sweet of you." No man had ever done such a nice thing for me before. It gave me the courage to ask, "What do all the experts agree on?"

"That talking about it in a safe environment can really help. I want to offer you that safe space to talk. We are not defined by our past. Understanding it goes a long way into being able to let go of it. Move on. Not let it affect the future. Apparently, the ultimate goal is forgiveness. That allows a person to take back their power."

We'd reached the police SUV and Ace opened the passenger-side door for me.

"Thanks. I appreciate that more than you know. And I will give that some real consideration." Though forgiveness seemed a bit out there. But taking my power back…? He had me intrigued there. If only it were so easy.

We drove back to town in silence. But why did she have to come back now of all times? So much going on with another murder investigation and me trying to figure my life out. I wasn't big on change. Maybe too much had happened to me as a child? Always moving and trying to stay ahead of creditors had sucked. *Big time.* But with all the money going for drugs and alcohol, what else could one expect to happen?

"Thanks for the lift, Ace. What do you want me to do for you? I can get readings on all the suspects."

He gave a huge put-upon sigh. "You're not going to be able to stay out of it, are you?"

"No." I shook my head for emphasis. My heart rate jacked up.

"Okay. I need to speak with the owner of the Inn next. Floyd Millhouse. We can hook up there."

"Thanks! You won't regret it."

"See that I don't."

I ignored his excessive enthusiasm and jumped down from the vehicle. *Wow.* A real step forward. After shutting the door to the SUV, I hurried into the café's kitchen.

"Granny, what are you doing here so bright and early?" I looked around, but she was the only person in evidence. It was only seven-twenty, so there was still plenty of time before we opened at eight for the breakfast crowd who enjoyed bakery goods in the morning.

"I wanted to check in on my favorite granddaughter."

I smiled at her kind words. Whichever one of us was near her at any given time was her favorite granddaughter. We all knew and appreciated the fact.

I kissed her soft cheek. "Want some tea?" Granny never drank coffee. She was an Earl Grey enthusiast through and through.

"Please. There's something we need to talk about."

My heart sank, knowing most likely what was coming. *More intel on my mother.* I filled the red metal kettle with water and set it to boil. After pulling out the teapot with the beautiful smiling face of a pixie as decoration, I rinsed it with hot water from the tap, added a pair of fragrant tea bags that stirred my senses, then sat down across from my beloved granny.

"Okay. Let's have it."

"Your mother's here."

I swallowed, not knowing what to say.

"She's at Auntie T.J.'s," she continued.

"Already? Have Tulip or Star seen her yet?" I drummed my fingers on the tabletop.

"No, not yet. She's resting after the journey. It would be best to wait until she's stronger. She's very tired. Auntie T.J. promised to call them this morning. I wanted to talk to you first."

"Okay." Waiting seemed like a good idea, even though a part of me wanted to get it over and done with.

"How are you doing, sweeting? I heard about your finding that man. How did that go?"

I shrugged, reliving the moment. "An odd thing happened. When I touched the man to check if he were alive, I got an image from him. A map."

"I see. Well, you're only twenty-one. Your powers will grow for years yet. The goddess blesses you when they're needed. The universe has order."

I smiled at her words. "Ace said the same thing this morning."

"You were out with your Mountie already today?"

"Yes, ma'am. He needed my help finding Sergei's ledger."

She nodded sagely. "Yes, of course. You two are a good pairing."

"Sometimes," I admitted. *Take my power back.* I liked that more and more. But forgiveness? That would be a tough one. I wouldn't know where to begin — so much crap had happened.

The kettle began singing and I jumped up to answer the call by pouring the boiling water over the teabags. Next step was to pop the lid back on and leave it to steep.

"Ace is a fine man and a very good lawman to boot."

"I know. Another strange thing happened. The map I saw? Kate Johnson also observed it being drawn onto her bathroom mirror by Sergei's ghost late last night. She came by earlier to ask me about it."

"A shared piece of evidence means it's of more importance. Can I see the map, please?'

I fetched my sketchpad, opening it to show her the drawing.

"That's some distance from here, through very rough terrain. You need to know that the importance of the vision gained through necromancy doesn't necessarily mean that one needs to go to the actual site. It may mean that the map *is* the connection to the murders."

"Makes sense." Though I appreciated the advice, I had to admit that a part of me was itching to head right out to Gold Mountain and find that X. It wasn't actually going to be painted in red for me on the ground, of course, but maybe I or one of my sisters had some stirrings of the divining gift that would allow us to find water or precious metal underground?

The door opened and in burst my two siblings, talking a mile a minute, and it didn't sound entirely friendly.

"Granny, Auntie T.J. just called and told us! And Star won't listen. Please explain that our mom needs us, and it's only right we visit her. I mean, she's our *mom*!" Tulip was more upset than I'd seen her in a long time.

"She doesn't care about us, for goddess sake! She's only here to make life more difficult for everyone. You know what she's like. I don't trust her, and I never will."

"Calm down, sweetings. You don't have to see your mother if you don't want to, Star. I only advise it because it means all of you can live without regrets. You have a lot of years to live yet, so you may want to come to some kind of closure for your childhood, painful as it was. But you don't have to. It's strictly up to each one of you. I'll support you either way."

Granny's wise words calmed the storm, but, by the mulish look on Star's beautiful face, she wasn't convinced of the necessity of not living with regrets. How did I feel about it? Granny and Ace had made important points. I'd need to think on it more.

"Time to open," I said, noting the clock. I couldn't take much more of this. "Who's watching the counter and who wants to bake today?"

"I'll bake. I don't feel like greeting everyone today." That was unusual for Tulip. She normally liked being out front, serving or working on her blog. Well, mostly working on her blog.

"I'll be in the front opening up if anyone needs me," Star said.

"Okay, that leaves me free to head out. I've got some people to interview about the murders."

"You have a list of suspects already?" Tulip asked as Star flounced from the kitchen.

"I do, and if you two can keep from killing each other today, I want to get right onto solving the case. Some people think that our auntie's to blame, and I can't have that."

"No kiddin'. Go. We've got this."

"Where will you go first, sweeting?"

"Ace and I are meeting up to speak with Floyd Millhouse this morning, so I've got to get going. He was seen with both of them. He might be able to shed some light on things." And it was better than starting with the other complicated situation with all the Hound's jilted lovers.

"It's good that you and Ace are becoming a team." She nodded approvingly. "You be careful, granddaughter. Take a protective amulet with you."

"Already taken care of." I patted the eagle talisman through my shirt. Grabbing my fall jacket, I thrust my arms into the sleeve and zipped it up to my chin.

"Catch you later." I kissed Granny on the cheek and gave Tulip a quick smile.

Chapter Twelve

The Lakeside Inn was a fair walk, being located on the highway outside of town, but I decided to hoof it anyway. I needed time to think. By the time I had reached the inn, I was less agitated, if no closer to knowing what I should do about my mother being in town. Was there a right way to deal with it that wouldn't drag up all the old damage from our childhoods? I doubted it. Growth was painful. And achieving forgiveness...? That had to be the most painful journey of all. *At least for this gal.*

I reached the Lakeside Inn and stopped for a moment to take in the well-maintained property. The styling of the two-storey structure was similar to Auntie's period-piece home, powder-blue siding with crisp white gingerbread trim along the eaves and gables, royal blue shingled roof, even a white picket fence separating the parking lot and sidewalk from the inn. I pushed open the frosted glass door and hurried over to the reception desk crafted of rich mahogany.

"Hi, Miss Betty," I said to the long-time employee with her steely-gray bun and starched white shirt. Its fancy dark-blue embroidered script on the pocket proclaimed her name. The signature matched in color to her blue skirt and shoes. Even Betty's crystal earrings matched. *Must be a strict dress code.* I didn't know Betty Rollins very well, though I was a bit cautious of her strong personality. She was nearing my auntie's age, having worked for Floyd for at least twenty-odd years. A spinster through and through, according to my auntie. A great reservoir of secrets no doubt, with her prominent position at the inn.

"Morning, Charm. I'll be with you in just one moment," she said, pleasantly enough. She was making an entry into the computer, a headset perched on her tightly pulled back hair. She finished keyboarding, pulled off the headset and turned to me with a professional smile. "How can I help you?"

"Actually, I was looking for Floyd. Is he around?" There was no sight of Ace yet, but I could at least go in and start the ball rolling.

"It's a bit early, but I'll check." She picked up the house phone and pushed a button. "Is Floyd around?"

She turned those quick bird-like eyes on me, listening to the person on the other end of the call, and I quirked my mouth into a smile.

She set the receiver in its cradle. "He's out back dealing with the groundskeeper. He'll be in shortly, if you'd like to wait?"

"Sure. So, I guess you're busy getting ready for the weekend?" I hadn't noticed many cars in the parking lot, so business must have been pretty quiet during the week.

"We are—booked up Thursday through Sunday, thank goodness. Snowy Lake can't have enough events in my opinion. Say..." She leaned forward and spoke so quietly I had to lean in to hear her. "You're the one that makes all the Promise Bags for the women for the Sadie Hawkins dance, right?"

I nodded. "I do. Were you interested in getting one made?"

Her pale skin flushed while she chewed on her bottom lip. "They can help encourage a man to do something for a woman that she wants, right? You put a spell on them?"

"Maybe a love spell is what you're wanting? To encourage the right man to speak up?" Intrigued, I gave her my best reassuring look.

"You can do that?" She turned pinker. She looked softer too, and if only she'd loosen the bun, she'd be far more attractive and approachable. *Should I say something?*

"Sure. I just need to know who you want to encourage. Of course, it only works if there is some mutual attraction already happening, however slight."

She frowned. "I'm not certain. I think so. I mean, he's always such a gentleman, but he has complimented me on a number of occasions."

"That's a good sign. Men do that when they want us to notice them — at least according to Granny."

"How is your granny?"

"Granny's fine, thanks for asking. So, what name shall I place on the spell in the Promise Bag? Will you be going to the dance?"

She leaned in even closer, her lips nearly brushing my ear. "William Bishop, please," she whispered. The name set me back on my heels. The very man I had planned to ask for Ivana. *Awkward or what?* I'd had no idea that Betty was interested in him. Bad Billy must be at least ten years younger than Betty, with a reputation that didn't make him seem her type at all.

"Bad Billy Bishop? You're quite certain?"

"Don't call him that! He's a lovely man."

"Of course, excuse me. How did you two meet?"

"I've known William for years. I was a few years ahead of him at school, but he was friends with my younger brother Ted."

A few years! "May I make a suggestion?"

"Of course."

"Susie Diamond at the Clip Joint's a great hairstylist, and when she does up a woman's hair and makeup, that can add magic. A lovely auburn tint and curls, and you'd be a new woman."

"You think so?" She held up her hands to her tight-threaded-gray bun, slicking back the one rebel hair that struggled valiantly to escape. "I don't know, Charm. Maybe I'm reaching too high, you know, trying to have William see me in a new light? Maybe I'm past all that?" The sadness that made her shoulders droop made me instantly want to do right by her, in any way I could. She needed more confidence, more belief in her abilities to attract a man. It was never too late, in my opinion. She had the right stuff. She just needed to project it better.

I nodded with enthusiasm, though I was now stuck looking for a new date for Ivana. "I'm *totally* convinced of it. She did my hair for a wedding this summer and I got noticed, let me tell you." It felt good to offer advice to Betty, like I was her long-lost girlfriend. We were all the same under the skin, looking for love and acceptance.

"Constable Ace Collins."

"Right, the new Mountie. You should have seen him fall at my feet when I walked in all dolled up for the first time. Susie's the real deal. Add one of my love charms to your Promise Bag, and you're good to go." Smug didn't cover it. It felt good to help her out.

"You misunderstand. I'm referring to the fact he's standing right behind you."

My heart fluttered. *No.*

I just didn't want to turn around. I wanted an invisibility spell to take me right the heck out of existence. I was consulting The Solomon Key grimoire for said spell — one I could enact at a moment's notice.

"Howdy, Miss Betty and Miss Charm," he said in an exaggerated southern drawl, letting his Kentucky roots show to full advantage. I studied my fingernails, observing that a manicure was very much needed, my polish non-existent. Maybe I should book an appointment at Susie's as well? *Then head on down to Doc Tanner's for a quick lobotomy.*

"What can I do for you, Constable Collins?" Betty asked, giving me a look of inquiry before her glance flitted back to Ace standing somewhere behind me.

"I'm needing to speak with Floyd Millhouse. Is he around?"

"Yes, I've already called him up for Charm. Ah, speak of the devil."

Interesting turn of phrase, 'speak of the devil'. I should have spent my time quizzing her about Floyd, not getting a serious case of foot-in-mouth disease. Why oh why had I said that about Ace? Awkward or what? Just when things were improving.

Floyd Millhouse looks a bit like a ferret with his brown pelt and close-set eyes. About a foot shorter than Ace and heavier set with a rotund belly, he'd been married to the same woman for twenty years, so that said something good about him, though his wife was one of those long-suffering types who brought me down if I spent more than thirty seconds in her company. She used to be a ray of sunshine, according to Granny, but I'd never seen any evidence of it.

"Morning, Constable Collins." He nodded at me, his eyes darting from Ace to Betty, his expression curious.

"I was wanting a word in private, Mr. Millhouse." Ace leaned down close to speak into my ear, whispering, "I'll go in first. Give me a few minutes, then make up an excuse to come in. Like Winn Duffy's looking for me."

I nodded, not daring to speak after my faux pas.

"Call me Floyd. We can head into my office." The inn's owner seemed unsurprised by our visit.

"I wonder what the constable wants with Floyd?" Betty asked, her expression perplexed as the pair vanished into the back room. "Do you think it has anything to do with those two recent deaths?"

I shrugged. "I imagine anyone who saw the two men over the weekend before they were found will be questioned."

"Floyd saw them? I didn't know that. Do you know where?" Betty leaned forward on the counter. Her eyes glittered with interest.

"At the Bowl-a-ram-a. Sean Blackmore saw them talking. Christine filled us in." I wasn't getting anywhere, fast, my tires spinning like I was doing wheelies in an empty parking lot. I swore I could smell rubber burning.

"Is something burning?"

"No, I don't smell anything."

Crap. That was the signal something bad was about to happen. "I should be going. I'll have that Promise Bag ready for you later today."

"Thanks, Charm. I appreciate it."

I pushed the frosted door open and headed into the sunshine, hoping to take a deep breath of for fresh air, but instead the rubber smell intensified.

Jogging down the road, I had a terrible sense of urgency.

Hurry! Help.

The words echoed in my brain. The odor of burning rubber became stronger. I increased my pace, a sense of foreboding making me queasy.

I pushed open to the door to the Tea & Tarot. Auntie T.J. barrelled toward me, her pink and bright red hair in complete disarray as she grabbed my arm.

Chapter Thirteen

"Charm! You're needed! She's *dying*," Auntie T.J. said.

Too stunned for words, I let her pull me back out through the door and down the street.

"Who's dying?" I asked. I swiveled my head around to see Star and Tulip close behind us, their faces tightened by worry.

She didn't answer but continued dragging me, digging her fingers into my arm.

"Where's Granny?"

"She's with her. We have to hurry."

At the end of Main Street, we turned north onto Telegraph Road and I knew. I jerked to a stop, just about pulling my auntie off her feet. "No! I'm not doing this."

"What? You have to! Hurry—we might be too late as it is."

"Charm, please," Tulip said, coming closer and placing her hand on my arm. "If we don't see her right now, we'll all regret it. We're bigger than that."

I could barely make any sense of the words coming from my triplet's mouth. When had Tulip gotten so wise? Those sentiments were not of the norm. They were goddess sent, the collective wisdom of the universe. Though I knew this, still, I fought it. Why didn't they just ask me to scale the highest mountain or swim the fastest river or fly to the moon? At least those activities I had a chance at getting through unscathed. Seeing my mother, knowing she was dying, I had absolute zero chance.

Star didn't say anything, her expression mirroring my own — mulish and upset to the nines. Her body was even levitating a few inches off the ground, something she only did when she was in an over-the-top emotional state.

"Sister hug," I said.

We huddled right there on the sidewalk, the three of us, outside Auntie T.J.'s house, and held on to each other for dear life. I gathered strength from the contact, holding on as long as they would allow it.

I swiped the tears from my cheeks, then reached up and dabbed at the ones leaking from Tulip's eyes, before wiping Star's away using a tissue from my pocket, being careful not to smear her pretty makeup. "Okay, we got this. We've the Invincible Trio." Both of my one-minute-younger siblings nodded, accepting my lead as they had always done. We high-fived for good measure.

"Let's roll." I threw my shoulders back and marched down the path that led to the house with my sisters flanking me.

Auntie T.J. followed along behind us, her expression, when I caught a glimpse of it, beyond proud, surprising me. It also gave me strength.

At the front door, my hand hovered over brass knob before I hardened my resolve and twisted it open.

The living room was dimly lit, but bells hummed softly in the background. It seemed all our protection spells were holding just fine. *You can do this, Charm.*

"She's in the guest bedroom. Do you want to go in together?" Auntie asked.

"I should go first." If anything could be done to help, it would be my job, my duty. I could spare my siblings that much at least.

"No! I'm going in," Star protested.

"Okay." I couldn't stop her and maybe it was for the best.

Like we were glued together, we shifted as one, making the condemned woman's walk to the guest room. The door was partly open, and through it I could see and hear Granny Toogood murmuring to a stranger. Shocked, I stumbled at the image of the woman on the bed, breaking free of my sisters at that instant. *No.* That wasn't our beautiful mother. The woman on the bed was shrunken, her graying hair limp and dank, her skin tone yellow.

I was the first to move forward, my sisters hesitating in the doorway. I approached the bed, the blood draining from my body. She looked so pitiful, so used up with her eyes closed that my heart squeezed at the sight. Were we too late? Was she already gone?

"Annie, your daughter Charm's here for you," Granny said. Granny looked at me, her expression saddened beyond measure.

The woman in the bed opened her eyes. She blinked a few times while staring at me like I might vanish at any second. I moved in closer to check her third eye, the one that appears when a person slightly blurs their own vision to see how another person is faring, leaning down to do so. It was so tired that it drooped between her other eyes, bloodshot and faded. Oh my, but she was ill...and perhaps beyond my help. "Charm, you're here. Thank you." She roused a bit, looking past me. "And your sisters have come as well."

The few words seemed to have tired her out and she closed her eyes again. I swallowed. Hard. This was far worse than I had expected. The woman who had been my mother in another lifetime was so thin that her body barely registered under the covers. Her birdlike wrists broke my heart all over again.

I slumped onto the bed and reached for her hands instinctively, though every cell in my body screamed at me to just walk away. To get out while I still could. It was all too much. Why now? Why was I being pushed so far so fast?

The connection between my mother and I intensified at that exact moment, and she moaned, pulling me in tight and making thinking difficult. I closed my own eyes, bowed my head, listening with all my being. A faint heartbeat! A body in peril. I collected all my energies and went to work. Time passed in a whirlwind, but I kept up my efforts to fix her, sending my healing energies down the pathways of her ailing body, though nothing felt like it was working. Was I failing now? When everyone else in the room was counting on me? *Oh goddess, give me the strength*, I prayed.

What was wrong? This healing should be similar to the two men who I had rescued from the ricin poison a few months back, because her kidneys were failing, poisoning her bloodstream the same as the poison had been doing to the stunt men from the movie set. But it was far more difficult. Was I too conflicted? Did I not want it enough?

I couldn't be that petty, could I? I had to rise above this. Be worthy. See her as a woman in need of my help, nothing more. Not good. Not bad. Just a human body requiring assistance.

Okay.

I reapplied myself, going back to the deep well of energy that existed inside me and pushing my fears, judgment, and pain away to stay neutral. *You can do this, Charm.*

It helped. Focused on healing the ill woman, I knew that at the very least I could buy her more time.

When I felt I could do no more, I sat back and gently pulled my hands away from hers. She didn't resist, just lay quietly.

"She'll sleep now," I said to the room, too exhausted to explain further. But I was fairly certain that I had done my best, even if it wasn't enough.

I stayed on the bed for a few minutes, too tired to get up. Granny reached over and touched my arm. "Are you okay, sweeting?"

"Really tired. But I'll be okay." At least I hoped so. The dark angel just couldn't be allowed to win. Not yet. We all needed more time to work through this. Not just me.

"Tulip, get your sister some juice," Granny said. Star and Auntie T.J. came closer to the bed while Tulip went to fetch the drink.

"She looks more peaceful," Star said, staring at the woman.

"Her color's better too," Granny said. "You did good, sweeting. I know that must have been hard for you."

I shrugged. My mouth was too dry to answer.

"Here you go," Tulip said, handing me a large glass of orange juice.

I gulped it down, so parched that I was certain we were stranded in the high desert. The juice trickled into my system, the natural sugars helping immediately. "Thanks."

"We should leave her to rest now," Granny said.

I got to my feet with a lot of effort that I struggled to hide, not wanting to look weak.

"I could use a sandwich. Anyone else hungry?" I asked.

"I've got the fixings in the kitchen," Auntie said, leading the way. With all of us housed around the large wooden table, the fun knickknacks of cats in funny poses that my auntie like to collect surrounding us, we fell into the normal way of things. Pretending that hard things didn't exist worked for us. *Most days.*

"Any idea of who I can get to be Ivana's date for Sadie Hawkins?" I asked, judging it time to think of lighter things.

"Ivana Petrov? *Our* Ivana!" Tulip looked astonished. Her eyes rounded like one of those famous big-eyed Margaret Keane paintings.

"The very one. I promised her a date, and Billy Bishop's taken. By Betty."

"*What?*" Star looked ready to levitate. "I don't believe it. Bad Billy and Betty Rollins?"

"Sweeting, don't be using that name. William's far more suitable," Granny said.

"Sorry. You're right, Granny. But, wow, I can hardly believe it." Star didn't look annoyed for once at being corrected. *Well, it helps if you're Granny Toogood. Me, she* just liked to blow off when she could, though, today, she'd come through when it mattered.

Now, this was what I would miss the most when she went to Hollywood—times around the kitchen table, just the family. Auntie T.J. was bustling about, rummaging in the refrigerator and assembling a platter of food on the counter. My stomach rumbled just thinking of it.

"I need ideas and I need them fast, people," I said, reminding them to stay on point. The clock was ticking quicker than a charge set to explode when the railroad was first built through the Canadian Rockies, because I knew darn well that if I didn't solve Ivana's dateless problem, I was doomed. Sharing Ace with her wasn't a proposition I would *ever* embrace.

"How about George Elliot?" Tulip asked.

"Yeah, maybe." I tapped my thumbnail against my front teeth. "I could check anyway. Any others come to mind?"

"I got nothing," Star said, shaking her head.

"I guess spelling him is out of the question," I said, hoping for a rise out of Granny.

"Sweeting! You know that's not ethical, not if he wasn't showing an interest as well."

"Maybe not, but it would be fun to try," Tulip said, coming to my rescue.

Granny corrected her with a look.

"Dig in." Auntie T.J. said as she set a tray of sandwiches and a basket of potato chips and other snacks on the table. She added a bowl of her famous brandied cherries for good measure.

Peace and quiet descended as we handed around the offerings and filled our plates. *Just another day in Snowy Lake.* Or at least, we were pretending it was.

Chapter Fourteen

"I need to head over to see if George Elliot's free on Saturday. You guys okay with holding down the fort for a bit longer?" I asked, as the three of us strolled down Main Street, our stomachs full.

"No problem," Tulip said.

"Thanks. I'll pick up Thor and head over to his farm right now, to see if he's around." George Elliot was a widower, a man in his early forties who farmed on the west side of town. The kind of man who knew his own mind...and maybe the kind of man to handle Ivana the way he handled his Wild Horse Ranch? He wasn't only an expert horse wrangler, but the winner of the Strongman of Snowy Lake contest three years running. That man could throw a bail of hay! He might be just the ticket to interest my wild Russian neighbor. At least I could dare hope. Marry Ivana off, and I'd get the top floor all to myself. Or maybe rent it out to a nice quiet librarian like Miriam?

"Do you think she's fixed — you know — healed?"

"I don't know, Star." I couldn't bear to tell her the truth.

"What do you mean? You always know. Didn't you do enough?" she asked, her eyes narrowed with indignation.

The very charge I had struggled with during my efforts to heal our mom dug at me more than I could say. Then I remembered Star had been the most hurt by it all. I recalled whispering to her in the dark, telling her that it would be okay, that I would be there for her. She'd always found it difficult, maybe more so than me, to deal with. It helped temper my response, just a little.

"I did my best! Pretended that the woman hadn't abandoned us and didn't give a sh—thing about us until she got sick! You saw how exhausted I was. I really, *really* tried. You have to believe me." Tears began streaming down my face of their own accord. Maybe I had held something back? My insecurity rose again, making me feel small and insignificant.

She nodded, her face morphing from anger and sadness in an instant. I felt bad for not telling her straight away, that though I had given our mother some strength, she was not healed entirely. Maybe enough to help her endure a kidney transplant? No, I didn't want to go there today.

"You did your best, sis. I saw that," Tulip said, handing me a tissue and patting me on the back. "Thank you for doing that. I know it must have been difficult. Not sure I could have done it."

I blew my nose and wiped my eyes.

"I'm sorry. I didn't mean to accuse you," Star said, her expression subdued.

"It's okay. I get it. I wasn't sure of myself for a bit there." I admitted a hard truth. "Not sure if I'm ever going to forgive what happened."

"I'll never forgive her!" Star said, that mulish expression back in full force.

We hugged again.

"Well, that's it then." I straightened my shoulders. *Time to grow a pair. Not like I haven't done it enough in the past.* "I'll see you both later."

We parted ways in front of the café, and I headed around the side of the building to the back where I'd parked Thor. I had a man to see about a horse. Oh, but first, I needed something to bribe him with. I scurried in the back door to the kitchen to see what treats were to be had. From the freezer, I retrieved a chocolate brownie layer cake with buttercream and toasted coconut topping, hauled it outside and placed it carefully on Thor's front passenger seat. *There, all set.* Or I would have been if a RCMP SUV wasn't blocking my path.

I groaned, sure of what was coming. I should have called him to let him know what had happened. That I hadn't meant to bail on helping with Boyd.

"Howdy, Sheriff, lovely to see you," I said, attempting a breezy tone. I really didn't want to get back to talking to him about the situation with my mother. I needed a little time to process it.

"Miss McCall." He touched the brim of his hat in that way he had that always made my insides feel quite unsettled, like they were in need of something. Today was no different. They quivered expectantly.

"I'm sorry I didn't wait at the inn to check out Boyd. Something came up."

"What?" he asked, his expression curious.

Fair question. I cleared my throat. "I got called away."

"Strangest thing. We're finally working on the same team, and you vanish. Not up to something, are you? Something you're hiding that you don't want me to know?"

"Not hiding a darn thing."

"Perhaps. But may I say in my defense how easy you make it for me to think that, considering your past shenanigans running around this town like you're the only one capable of solving a crime? I'm not doing that anymore, Charm. I want us on the same page here. If you got something to say, just spit it out."

"No, I'm good."

"I would like to finish this business with Boyd right now, if you can spare a few minutes?"

"Right now? I was just on my way to talk to George at Wild Horse Ranch about the Sadie Hawkins dance."

"Really? I thought I had the honor of being your date?" His expression changed in a heartbeat.

"An honor, is it? Yeah, well, Ivana needs a date or she'll home in on ours. Apparently, wants herself quote, a 'Hero Sandwich'."

His eyes grew a size larger. "If you need help persuading him, let me know. I'm sure we can find something or drum up something to encourage his active participation as her guest."

I pursed my lips to keep from bursting into laughter. "No woman scares any man more than our Ivana, eh!"

He snorted. "I refuse to answer that on the grounds it might incriminate me. But if you have a few minutes right now, I'd be happy to accompany you over to the Lakeside Inn."

"Okay, but I'll follow you over there in Thor, then head out to the ranch and talk to George. I've got a chocolate brownie layer cake with buttercream and toasted coconut topping with his name on it. I hope it's enough."

"It would be if Miss Petrov was your average woman. But she's a far cry from that. You might want to up the bribe."

"You had any personal dealings with her?"

He turned red under his tan and I gritted my teeth. *What did she do?* If she'd stepped over the line, she'd hear about it, Bratva brothers or not. *No one touches my Mountie and gets away with it.* "Ace, did she do something I need to know about?"

Nice to know she cares so much.

He was turned away from me as I heard the words and I couldn't get a read on him. "Did you say something?"

"No, nothing. It's fine. Let's go. I need answers — yesterday."

"Okay, then." I jumped into Thor and started his motor, careful to drive in a less flashy manner than usual behind Ace's police cruisier all the way to the inn. It just about killed me.

I parked Thor alongside Ace's vehicle and jumped out. We strode to the front doors together and my Mountie opened it like the gentleman he had proven to be to date.

"You're back," Betty said, surprised.

"Is Floyd still out back?"

"No, he's in his office. Shall I get him for you?" Her glance darted back and forth between us, like she was she was calculating what it meant, our appearing together like this so soon after our last visit.

"We'll just head in if that's all right?" Ace said.

"Sure. Go right ahead. Are we still on for later, Charm? I'll need to pay you for your time," Betty said.

"Yes, but make it closer to suppertime. I've got some errands to run."

"That's fine." She nodded vigorously, her bun too stacked and cemented in place to dare move. I itched to help her out, but Susie Diamond was better equipped.

Ace nodded at her and strode off down the hall, making me jog double-time to keep up with his far longer strides.

Ace knocked briskly on the door marked *Office*. He turned the doorknob and entered the instant he heard Floyd shout out, "Come on in."

The second that it registered on Floyd who he had just invited in, his expression shifted and tightened. That intrigued me. Just running into the law could cause that look, or was it something else?

"Constable Collins, what a surprise. I wasn't expecting you back so soon." Floyd didn't get up but leaned forward in his black office chair and pointed at the chairs in front of his desk. "Have a seat."

"How are you, Floyd? It's been a while," I said, settling down in a chrome chair beside Ace.

"Yes, it has. How's your family? Granny Toogood's doing well, I hope?"

I nodded, trying not to let my smile slip at thoughts of earlier today.

Floyd looked at Ace. "So, what can I do for you? I thought we'd covered it all earlier, Constable?" He glanced at me, like he didn't want to say more in my presence.

The silence grew unbearable.

"New evidence has popped up," I jumped in. "A treasure map that points to Gold Mountain."

Floyd's eyes turned more ferret-like, if that were possible, turning into cold marbles. "Has an actual map been found?"

"I made a copy of it." I fudged my answer. Explaining a map that had only been found in my mind and drawn from memory would be hard to do and not helpful in this situation.

"You found the original?" His eyes bore into me.

Now why did he have to go and ask that?

"Mr. Millhouse, were you aware of this map?" Ace got right to the point.

"*Phtttt*, treasure maps are a dime a dozen in the north. You got to Dawson City in the Yukon and you can get your hands on a whole slew of them. Ever heard of Suspicion Mountain in Arizona and the Lost Dutchman Mine? It's a cottage industry all over North America."

Cagey answer, buddy.

"You didn't answer my question," Ace said.

"Do you have the map, Constable?"

"What's important here is whether you were aware of the map's existence?"

"I'd have to see it to know if I've ever seen it before." Floyd shrugged. "It's been a decade or more since I've had an interest in gold mining."

Interesting. "Did you ever pan for gold near Gold Mountain?" I asked.

"What's this go to do with anything?" Floyd asked. "I thought you were investigating a murder connected to moonshine, not gold mining?"

"Would you be willing to undergo a lie detector test of sorts? Eliminate yourself as a suspect?" Ace asked.

"I've done nothing wrong and have nothing to hide. I don't need to prove it to anyone but myself, Constable."

"The law might beg to differ."

I got up and slipped around the side of the desk. It was obvious I had carte blanche from Ace with his 'lie detector of sorts' comment. I reached for an item on the shelf of knickknacks just above my sight line.

"This is cool." I pretended to lose my balance and let myself fall against Floyd, using a hand to right myself on his shoulder. I closed my eyes and took a quick reading.

An image came to mind. *Eww.* The man was thinking about me! I dropped my hand instantly and placed the trinket of the Las Vegas strip back on the shelf, then scooted around the desk and sat back down beside Ace, trying not to let my feelings show.

Ace gave me a quizzical look that I ignored, pasting a smile on.

"Was there anything else, Constable?"

"Yes, don't leave town."

"No problem there. This is my town, lived here since I was twenty-five. Suits me just fine." His smarmy tone suggested that his longer residency trumped Ace's recent transfer to Snowy Lake.

Floyd was the beneficiary of one last I've-got-my-eyes-on-you-look from Ace before we exited the office.

In the parking lot, Ace turned to me. "What did you see?"

I rolled my eyes. "Well, let's just say we have a new town Hound Dog to replace Sergei."

His eyes narrowed, his jaw tightened and he looked suddenly ready to head back into the inn, guns blazing.

I put out a hand to stop him. My, he had well-developed biceps "It's okay. Wasn't that bad. I'll just have our coven make poppets and set him right."

A grunt followed my words.

"Maybe a pin poked into a sensitive area wouldn't be amiss," I suggested and earned a chuckle this time for my efforts.

"You are incorrigible, Miss McCall."

"I aim to please."

"Charm, there's something else I wanted to say." He paused.

"Yes?"

"I heard that your mother's back in town sooner than expected. How are you doing?"

"All right, I guess." I swallowed and looked away. The very thing I wanted to avoid. *Discussing my mom.* But maybe it was best to just get it over with since it was already out there. "I—I tried healing her this morning. That's where I went earlier, but no dice. Maybe bought her a little more time, is all."

"I'm sorry to hear that."

I ventured a quick glance at Ace and saw the sympathy for me on open display. "Well, there are things the universe can't fix. Her kidneys are on borrowed time."

"I very much want you to be okay with all this. Did you get a chance to talk with her at least?"

"No." I shook my head vehemently, hearing the rawness in my tone. "She was too ill."

"Well, she's better now, right? Maybe you can settle things in your mind if you have some time alone to talk with her? Hear what she has to say? Before it's too late, you know."

"Maybe." I really didn't want to talk about it anymore. But I also didn't want to upset Ace. I felt his good intentions in his every word. Maybe I was incapable of following them, but I wasn't going to say that out loud. And just maybe, I would find it in my heart to give it a try. *Soon.* Before it was too late. Because that was the scariest part of it all. Time was running out.

Ace shifted his stance and the moment passed. "Okay, I'll let you get on with arranging a date for Miss Petrov. I think that should be set to high priority."

"As do I, Constable. Catch you later." I waggled my fingers in a cute wave and jumped into Thor. "Okay, we got a mission to accomplish."

Chapter Fifteen

Wild Horse Ranch. The name was carved into a large piece of whitened driftwood hung between two debarked trees, then strung across the graveled entrance way to George Elliot's thousand acres. I turned off the main road and drove under the sign, keeping a look out for wildlife...and George's fabled menagerie of chickens, goats and barking dogs.

The large, white-framed farmhouse and accompanying huge red barn came into view around a bend in the narrow road, a lazy drift of wood smoke swirling out of the fieldstone chimney. I spied George's black Ford half-ton in the yard along with Eric Taylor's shiny red GMC with the fancy chrome wheels that made it easy to identify. *Nice.* Eric was on my suspect list, and being a moonshiner too, of keen interest to *moi.*

I parked nearby, picked up the fancy cake and jumped to the ground. No horses in evidence, but I imagined they were still out to pasture. The sound of voices drew my attention to the machine shed on my left, opposite the barn, and I took off at a trot, past the house and down the narrow path that led to the wide-open doorway.

Both men looked over at me with surprise when I popped inside and offered up a greeting. The distinct smell of grease and gasoline assailed my nostrils, a familiar odor from all the farms and ranches in the area that housed and maintained their own farm equipment. I spied a ubiquitous green John Deere tractor and a bailer needed for cutting winter feed for the horses, along with a selection of smaller pieces all lined up in a tidy row.

George came right over to greet me, while Eric hung back and watched. George is a big man, good-looking, his tan skin a bit weathered by endless days under the hot prairie sun. His ballcap hid a thick mane of prematurely silver hair that offered distinction to his solid profile. Bright blue eyes bore into mine with confidence and I offered up a smile in response. George was easy to like.

"Mornin', George. I come bearing gifts." I held out the cake box and he smiled at me as he observed the cellophane see-through cover that exposed the top of the dessert.

"Say, is that one of those fine chocolate brownie layer cakes with buttercream and toasted coconut topping from the Tea & Tarot?"

"It is. Fresh-baked yesterday and flash-frozen, so as soon as it's thawed, which it pretty much is now, you can dive right in. And there's more where that came from."

His eyes twinkled with good humor. "So, what do I owe the honor, Miss McCall? I assume you have a trade in mind?"

George was a very savvy man and would be a good catch for some lucky woman. He was well-liked for caring to the proper needs of his horse herd, his volunteer efforts in helping young people by coaching hockey and for his good business head. My pulse quickened. What I had to ask was a doozy. I hesitated, desperately wanting to have my wish granted. I was running out of time with the event only days away.

"Actually, you caught me. I do have a favor to ask." I glanced over at Eric, who had come closer, intrigued by what was in the bakery box, by his lingering looks. The man obviously loved food — only five-foot-eight in his boots, he was at least as wide again, all top weight on thinnish legs clad in too-tight jeans.

"Well, ask away. If it's in my realm to help you, I will grant it. Of course, then I may ask you for a future favor in return?"

I nodded, hoping it wasn't something too difficult or off-the-wall. It wouldn't be the first time asking for Ivana had left me in the soup. Or more accurately, this time it would be cake batter, as I would need to replace the cake I had snaffled from the freezer. "Of course, fair's fair."

"It's about Ivana Petrov."

His eyes widened before they narrowed to a slit, the blue vanishing in an instant. "What about her?"

I swallowed. *Oh-oh.* What had she done to fabulous George? "You know it's Sadie Hawkins this weekend?"

He made the connection and his lips firmed into a straight line.

"But, if the woman's too much for a big man like you to handle..." I left it hanging and prayed he'd take up the challenge.

"What? You can't handle her, George? Heck, give me that cake, a promise of a future favor and I'll take you up on the offer," Eric said with aplomb.

I gifted Eric with a wide smile and thrust the box at him. He might have been a heavy-set man, but he was light on his feet when it came to dancing. And Ivana loved to dance. "Thank you for stepping up. We appreciate your support. There's more cake where this came from. Just keep the deal from Ivana, please. That's all I ask."

"No problem there. My lips are sealed."

"Thank you."

"*Hey*, wait a darn minute, I didn't say I *wouldn't* do it," George protested. "Give a man a chance to answer, why don't you? Yes, I'll take you up on the challenge. That little filly's been needing a real man for a while."

I kept the smile pasted on my face, only imagining what Ivana would think of being called a *little filly*. I swallowed my fear, just visualizing it. But then, maybe being fought over would entice her. And George was normally a perfect gentleman, when he wasn't feeling one-upped by Eric.

"I'll see to it that you get a cake too, Eric. My way of saying thanks," I said, reaching to take the cake back. But something odd was going on, for he held on to the box for dear life, refusing to hand it back. *Hmm.* Had we overdone the Kismet Spell? But it did offer the perfect opportunity.

I touched his forearm to reassure him. "Really, I'll bring another cake over to your house today, I promise." A zinger of an image traveled from him to me as I spoke. Eric was thinking that when he got his hands on the gold, he'd buy all the cakes he wanted. An image of the treasure map was obvious in his mind.

My shock must have shown on my face, because Eric's eyes turned calculating. He still had the cake clutched to his chest as if it were the gold he sought.

"What's up, Charm? What did you see?"

"Nothing." I shook my head, nervous all of a sudden. So, Eric knew of my ability and believed in it. I'd had no idea. "Well, I should be going. I've got to work today."

"I'll see you out," George said.

Our boots crunched on the gravel as we traversed the walk back to my Jeep together. I hurried along beside him, feeling uncomfortable with Eric watching me from behind. I wanted to turn right around and cast out a zinger of a protection spell, but I stopped myself. It would be a mistake to let on what I had learned. He was now my number one suspect in the murders. He wanted gold as much as he lusted after cake.

"I'll bring another cake by later," I said when we reached Thor.

"Thanks, I'd appreciate that. I don't think I'll be seeing any of that one any time soon." George chuckled.

"And thanks for being Ivana's date. 'Bless your heart', as my granny would say."

"Well, it should prove interesting, if nothing else. Just tell me her Promise Bag won't house something too insurmountable for this humble rancher. I've always suspected they're spelled or bewitched in some way, right?"

I winked at him, my equilibrium fully restored. There was even more to George than I had realized. Was he the elusive match for Ivana I had been searching for? "I can do that, since I'm in charge of preparing them. They'll be no obligation for you to bow to any of her wishes. You're a good man, George Elliot."

I jumped into Thor, gunned the motor and headed us back into town. Humming along to the radio, I parked in front of the Loonie Bin where everything cost only a Loonie or two, Snowy Lake's own version of a dollar store.

"Morning, Josie," I said. She was busy assembling a new display of Halloween items, from kitchen witches riding straw brooms to wall decorations of goblins and ghosts. Hmm, I still needed to have a serious talk with baby Ling Ling to name that ghost.

"Morning, Charm." She returned my greeting with unexpected enthusiasm, considering her recent lover had met his demise. Her thick blonde hair was stylishly fashioned into a flattering bun, her eyebrows groomed to the nines. *What is it about eyebrows lately?* I raised a hand to my own, wondering if I had been missing the mark. Maybe I should consult Star? She was always up on the best trends. "What can I help you with?"

Hmm, what did I need? "Love your display, by the way. One can't have enough Halloween decorations."

"Oh, I know! I love Halloween. Look at this." She held out a teeny-tiny witch riding a pen flashlight. "Isn't that adorable?"

"Form and function, eh." I held out a hand to take the item from her, appreciating the perfect opportunity to gain a reading. When our fingers touched, I received a jolt. *Her happy face? Fake, fake, fake.*

"I was so sorry to hear about Sergei. Terrible thing." I watched her face carefully. A micro-expression of intense anger exposed itself for a split second before it was buried deep.

"Yeah, I wonder what killed him? Was it something in the moonshine like everyone's been saying?"

"I haven't heard." I shrugged. "I didn't realize you two had broken up?"

She narrowed her eyes at me. "That was a while back. Unfortunately, he lived up to his reputation. I should have listened."

"Well, he did have a very charming way about him."

"Yeah, he did." She reached into her box of items and drew out a classic white ghost-on-a-string with a special lightbulb attached at the back to make it glow in the dark.

"Oh, I need one of those."

She handed it to me with a nod. "Here ya go."

I checked the price tag. Nice, only cost two Loonies. "Thanks. Did Sergei ever talk about a goldmine?"

"Goldmine? No, never heard him mention anything like that. Why?"

"I was just wondering. Some evidence I'm really not at liberty to discuss."

"Harrumph." She looked less pleased now and turned her back on me to work on the display.

"But I can share that there's a treasure map involved."

She whirled around. "Really? That's awesome. Do you think it has anything to do with the Altima people that are coming back in the spring?"

Not again. As soon as she said Altima, another vision rose in my mind of she-who-shall-not-be-mentioned. "Are you going to the Sadie Hawkins dance?" I hadn't received any requests from her. She was single and available.

"Nah. I've given up dating for the foreseeable future. Once burned, twice shy."

Josie was giving off such weird vibrations that I was keeping her on the suspect list. *For now.* Maybe it was exactly as she said, and her anger was justifiable in that she'd been jilted by Sergei. But I hadn't heard of any other woman after her, and the Hound Dog had always had a woman on his arm. Was she trying to cover up her involvement in someway?

"Did you know of any other woman he was seeing?"

She leaned in close and hissed. "Kate Johnson, last I heard."

Did I have my facts wrong? Or was she reinventing history? "Did you see them together recently?"

She rolled her eyes. "I don't like to speak of it. I mean, she's married, right?"

Good ball lob. But why? If she had no involvement with the murder or murders, why did she need to reinvent the story? None of that made any sense to me. There were too many suspects and I needed more concrete facts.

"I wouldn't be too hard on them right now. There are things going on you don't know about." *Like Kate seeing ghosts and drinking too much.*

"No worries." She grimaced and put out another flashlight witch on the shelf.

"Would you like me to check your health? Since I'm right here." I wanted badly to take a full reading on her, to get into her mind and discover the truth.

"I feel fine. Better than ever, really." She dismissed my words and dug around in her goodie box, dragging out a change purse with a happy witch riding her broom across the sky.

"I'll take that one."

She handed it to me.

"Everyone thinks they're fine until they aren't. And not like it's going to cost you anything," I pressed. "You can't get a better deal than that."

She looked undecided and I sent a little encouragement her way, asking the goddess for forgiveness for the intrusion.

"Okay. Why not? Not like you're charging me anything and it never hurts to know more about yourself, right?"

She held out her hands and I eagerly took them in mine.

"Close your eyes, please." Visions of a slideshow winked in quick succession across her mind, too quickly for me to keep up, though I did catch a couple. Josie wanted more, so much more than she had looking after a chronically ill mother and feeling trapped in Snowy Lake.

"You have an amazing brain."

"Thanks."

"You bought liquor from Sergei on Sunday." We both knew she did, but I needed to see the interaction.

"What of it? I dumped it after I got the warning from you. Besides, it wasn't even for me." She wanted to pull her hands away. I held on. A flash of Sergei in Skull Cave entered her brain. She was flirting with him then he said something about another woman. She spit on the ground at his feet, then stomped away, holding a liter jar of Apple Pie Moonshine. No man was ever going to take advantage of her ever again. As soon as she could, she was moving on. And the moonshine was for her mom.

"You're in good physical shape, no obvious problems with your health," I said.

"Thanks. My momma taught me that no matter what happens, it's important to look after yourself. Keep up appearances. No way was I going to weep over that snake-in-the-grass. All his talk of having changed, wanting to be a better man. Wanting to make me his queen. Baloney."

"I understand. And I really admire your attitude." The reading and her words explained so much. "Ever thought of checking out our coven, the Northern Lights, as my guest? You might like it. And you're just the kind of woman we need. Independent and you think for yourself."

I had made an about-face here, but I could see she hadn't been involved in his death, having discovered his new indiscretion too late in the day to have poisoned his moonshine, and that she'd had no such intention in the first place. Thank goodness I was a stickler for the truth and had pushed the envelope to the max today. It had paid off, big time. The fact that she read and loved Agatha Christie didn't hurt her cachet one bit.

"Maybe I will." She pursed her lips, considering. "When's your next meeting?"

"I'll call you with the date and time. After the meeting, which usually includes a magic demo or practice, we also watch a movie for fun. Each member takes turn bringing the snacks."

"That sounds rather nice. Sure, I'll take up on it."

"Great. I'll be in touch." I wanted to keep an eye on her though I had not sensed any evil intentions in her. *You are a very unusual person, Josie Davidson.* I could even see asking for her help one day. She had an exceptionally high IQ, ready-made for puzzles. And with Snowy Lake teeming with them of late, I wanted a mind like hers on our team.

Chapter Sixteen

I pushed open the door of the Tea & Tarot café, pleased with myself. I had important intel to share with Ace that would benefit our investigation. I had all but forgotten what had happened earlier, but one look at Tulip and her red-rimmed eyes and it all came flooding back.

"Everything okay, sis?" I asked, rushing over to check on her. She was slumped over her computer, her fingers idle. As much as her choice to work on the computer over hard labor irked me on occasion, today I'd prefer to see her happily click-clacking away, sending out her positive, endearing messages to the world.

She sighed. "I don't know. Today's been so weird."

"Any news I should know about?"

"Mom's doing better. Doc Tanner said whatever you did, it helped her. But she's not healed, right?"

"No. I'm sorry, sis." But had I really tried enough? It was the kind of thing I'd always question now. Gifts came with a cost. That kind of sucked.

Tulip nodded, her tears spilling over.

"Hey, it's okay, kiddo." I hugged her, tears prickling behind my eyelids again. "But at least we've bought her more time."

"I talked with her this afternoon after she rallied. She's really sorry and wants to make it up to us." Tulip slumped against me.

"I'm sure she is. And probably wants a kidney to boot." I head the dryness in my tone and I swallowed. *Oh boy, such mixed-up feelings.* I wanted to escape and get back on the case. At least that I could control. I most wanted to see this goldmine everyone was so in awe of.

"Would that be so wrong?"

"What's that, sweeting?" I absently stroked her back, my mind far off at the base of Gold Mountain. If I got up early, I could make the journey in one day. Or maybe take camping gear just in case. A great deal of the trip would have to be on foot, and that would take time, so rather hard to estimate.

"You're not even listening!" She pulled away angrily and dried her eyes.

"I'm sorry." I sighed. "You're right. I was thinking about the recent rash of deaths. I've been working on figuring out what happened all day."

"Did you learn anything?" Her expression shifted.

"Some interesting things." I shared what I knew just before an intense urge over came me and I grabbed for a pen and paper, scribbling down the words—

Dragon's breath, life and death, come to me
Things seen and things unseen,
Let me walk here between.

I stared at my words from the automatic writing. *Oh goddess*. This was a spell of the highest order. Something was brewing in the universe. Something *huge*.

"What is it?" Tulip looked over my shoulder.

"We should expect company or a call at any moment."

"What does it mean?"

"It's from the days of Merlin. A spell to cloak. Invisibility." How I knew that, I wasn't certain, but a sense of going up to a new level was upon me and that I did not question. There was need for this spell somewhere in the universe and it had been handed to me. I would know in the proper moment when to share it. *And with who.*

"Really? You can do that? I wonder who needs it?"

"I don't know. But it will only work if the need is real and honest and the universe deems it of enough importance to charge it."

"Wow. That's rather mind-blowing." Tulip gave me a strange look, like she didn't quite know me.

"I'm just the conduit. The universe gives it the power, not me."

The angel chimes over the door began singing to high heaven, announcing a visitor of renown. *Ah.* Constable Ace Collins strode in, a man on a mission.

"Constable." I smiled, enjoying the view.

He came straight over. "We need to talk."

"Of course. I have a lot to share too. Coffee? Food?"

"Coffee would suffice. I don't have much time unfortunately."

I poured us coffees and handed him one. Tulip discreetly took off, leaving us alone. I was pleased to see she looked better. Our strange conversation had taken her mind off our family troubles. I'd do just about anything to keep my mind clear of it as well.

"So, spill, darlin'. I can see you're dying to tell me what you discovered on your travels today."

"Oh yeah? Maybe I'm just happy to see you?"

"That so?" He grinned over the rim of his cup before taking an appreciative sip of the fragrant brew. Now that we had learned to work better together — this was our third go-around with murder investigations, after all — Ace had been busting my chops less often. "Well, you are my favorite amateur sleuth."

"I'm hardly an amateur!" I protested. "I do have an honorary RCMP badge, special-built." It was one pay grade above Ace's to boot. *Sweet.*

"Don't remind me. And I still have it locked away in a desk drawer where it won't be seeing the light of day anytime soon. Have I told you you're incorrigible yet today?"

His lips looked so plush as they curved into a teasing smile. "Yes. Have I told you that you're a traditional stick-in-the-mud type who's afraid of a little honest competition?"

"I'm immune these days, darlin'. I know you too well to take offense. You like, *like* me."

"How can you be so sure?" I raised a coy eyebrow at him and set my cup down on the counter.

"I can see it in your eyes. You want me to kiss you." He punctuated his remarks by setting his own cup down, then leaning toward me and bestowing a kiss on my waiting lips. An awesome kiss that made my insides flutter. He tasted of coffee and mint, his outdoorsy wind-and-sky scent mixed with earthy leather and fragrant soap. I sighed. I loved the way he smelled. The elixir seemed more intoxicating by the day, with more and more overtones.

This time when the kiss ended, he placed a friendly arm across my shoulders and tugged me closer to his warm body. I fit in the crook of his arm like I was custom designed to be there.

"I want to tell you what I learned today." I shared the facts of my interviews with Eric Taylor and Josie Davidson. I left out my need to visit the goldmine. There was no point in bothering him with that until I knew more.

"That's helpful. I also got back the results of the autopsies. Safe to say, this is a murder investigation. Those men did not die of natural causes."

"It's a complicated case. That much I know."

"Having two bodies makes discovering the motive all that more imperative. I don't want any more deaths on my watch." His expression darkened. Ace had totally adopted our town as his own. "The goldmine is key. I need to discover the connections between the two men over that treasure map. And where that map is now."

"Hmm."

"What? No ideas?"

"I was just thinking about ghosts and goldmines and what a double aura means. Tulip saw one on Floyd. First one she's seen. Made me think of our last case with one of the suspects having a split personality."

"*Our case* is it, now?" He smiled.

I lightly punched his arm. "You need me more than you know."

"Aw, that I do, darlin'." He moved closer just as the door opened, causing a wild ruckus of discord from the angel chimes.

I whirled around to observe Ivana Petrov coming into sight, her expression wilder than the angel chorus had been. I swallowed, thankful I had good news for her.

"Lawman and best friend." Her expression shifted as she came closer. "Did Charm tell you news?"

"What news, Miss Petrov?" Ace remained calm. He was gifted.

"We make Hero Sandwich."

"No! I've got you a date, Ivana. A *great* guy. I think you'll like him. He's a local rancher." Frantic to head her off at the pass, I grabbed my cell phone and brought up George's photo of him riding a black stallion on a fine summer day. If our cell phones were mostly useless due to the poor reception, at least they made decent time pieces and photo holders.

"Aw, like Putin. Nice. But Hero Sandwich —" She laid a hand on Ace's forearm and squeezed. "Big loss."

"Ivana, it's Romeo and Juliet. Not Romeo and Juliet and Juliet and Juliet." I tried giving her a visual to help her see the big picture.

Of course, it worked about as well as anything I explained to her. "Who this extra woman? You like large harem, big man?"

Ace turned a dull shade of red. "No, can't say that suits. I'm strictly a one-woman-one-man man." He sounded a bit tongue-tied as he laid it out.

"Big loss for you. But good, George and horse. He ride with me. Bare-chested."

"Excellent." I took a deep breath, vowing not to dig deeper into her last comment and find out exactly *who* was going to be bare-chested. "That's settled then." I would have the Mountie all to myself.

Ivana click-clacked across the floor, vanishing from view.

"Not sure I want to be compared to Romeo and Juliet, considering the ending to that tale," Ace said.

"Then how about Orpheus and Eurydice? Would you travel to the underworld to rescue me?" I teased, wondering if he knew the story. Ace was well read and often surprised me.

"Hardest part would be in not looking back at you."

I blushed from the roots of my hair to the tips of my toes.

"That's the most romantic thing I've ever heard anyone say." I held my hand over my heart. Suddenly nervous, I searched around for something, anything. "I should get to baking some cakes. Bribery is depleting our stock."

"And I should be getting back as well. I'll catch you later." He tipped his hat as I nodded. "I'd rescue you from anywhere. Hades, if necessary." And with that, he made his departure, leaving me in a state of frustrated bliss. And darn if the sensation wasn't becoming more common these days. *Time to whip up some cakes and take my mind off the lawman.*

I hurried into the back of the café and went to work. In short order, I had cake batter as far as the eye could see, and the kitchen was filled with the heavenly fragrance of caramelized sugar, toasted coconut and vanilla beans. I even had the kitchen to myself, and I was not complaining. Baking was my go-to occupation when I needed a timeout. There was something very satisfying about the measuring process, the stirring of ingredients and the best thing, the final delectable results. *Happy smiles optional.*

When the final cake was Kismet blessed and tucked in the freezer, the last dish washed and stacked in the cupboards and my stomach overfilled with cake batter and coffee, I headed upstairs. I'd even managed to finish the Promise Bag for Betty in the midst of all the activity and she'd dropped by to pay me.

As I slipped between the freshly laundered sheets while breathing in the soothing fragrance of Downy, Ling Ling jumped up and settled down next to me.

"Tomorrow you and I are having a *long* talk, missy," I warned her before turning out the bedside lamp. I also needed to do the same with my auntie at the first opportunity. She'd been MIA all day. *Figures.*

I think I fell asleep before my head actually made contact with the pillow, because the next thing, I knew I was being jerked awake by a sudden noise. Where was it coming from? I checked the beside clock. *Yikes*, I was running late and it was likely one of my sisters hard at it downstairs in the kitchen...or just making noise so I'd get up and do the job for them. Tulip and Star were not quite the helpers they imagined themselves to be. Though, to be fair, they had both been stepping up more this past year, especially since Granny had reminded them that *'excuses accuse no one but yourself, sweetings'*. Wise woman.

I jumped in the shower, dried off then dressed in a navy-blue long-sleeved Henley tee and dark wash jeans, pulling my hair up into a high pony. If I were going to head off for a long hike, there was no point in getting dressed up. I stopped in mid-action, my hands still holding up my hair. When was the last time I hadn't seen Ace once or ten times in a given day? How was I going to keep him from heading right off after me when he was needed here in town far more? Not to mention that I desperately needed some alone time to think away from recent events with my mother and checking out the goldmine was the perfect opportunity.

Stymied, I studied my reflection in the bathroom mirror, noting my irises were still as pansy-colored as Elizabeth Taylor's, not that I had been taking the time to enhance them with makeup of late. *This weekend,* I promised myself. *I'll get all dolled up for the dance.* I suddenly realized I had the perfect excuse — a day spent with Susie Diamond at the Clip Joint. I made a quick call and booked a real appointment for Saturday, finding it a bit awkward to ask for the second favor. But she cheerfully agreed to cover for me. Susie was a real gem. She often encouraged women to enjoy a time out in her awesome salon, secure in the back room that she'd stocked with novels, loungers and afghans for comfort. The fact that I wasn't actually going to be in attendance didn't faze her at all.

I bounced downstairs, taking the steps two at a time, not worried so much about waking Ivana now that I had solved the dicey situation. Star was making coffee at the counter and looked over, her expression sad.

"Morning, lazy bones," she said. Though she was yanking my chain, I kept the retort inside. Yesterday had taken its toll on my siblings, and I wasn't prepared to get on her case this early in the day.

"Morning, sis." I grabbed a couple of white mugs with the fancy red Tea & Tarot logo from the metal tree stand, added a dash of cream to each then handed her one. She filled her cup then tipped the pot over mine. "Thanks. I need to talk with you."

"Yeah, me too."

We sat down across from each other at the table.

"So, what's up?" she asked, watching me over the rim of her cup.

That surprised me. Star usually launched into her spiel first off, but I was not going to lose the advantage. "I need to check out a clue today and might not make it back tonight. Can you cover for me? Say I'm over at Susie's having the works, if the constable should happen by?" I felt a considerable twinge at the deceit. It wasn't my usual MO, especially now that we were working together and I worried I was inviting bad karma with the fib, but I felt it was necessary. This wasn't hiding intel from him but going off to discover if there was more to be had. *Big difference*, I reassured myself.

"Where are you going? What clue?"

"Going to check out a treasure map. I'll be fine."

"Not like anyone could stop you anyway," she muttered.

"What's that supposed to mean? I'm doing it for the good of all of us. We need to get to the bottom of the murders, and Ace is needed right here in town." *And I need time alone to think things through.*

"Whatever." She shrugged, then chewed on her bottom lip. "But you will be careful, right? Gold Mountain's got a reputation."

Which reminded me. "Shoot, did baby Ling Ling leave already?"

"Yeah, I fed her just before you came down and she took right off."

"Probably doesn't want to be put on the spot about the ghost she saw the other day." I shook my head and took a satisfying gulp of my coffee. I had preloaded the coffee machine last night, so all Star had had to do was turn it on. How had that activity caused such a clatter? There was no evidence of any work being done yet.

"I wanted to tell you this first. If Mom needs a kidney, I'll do it."

Her words hit me hard. So hard that I set my cup down with a loud thud, coffee spilling over. I was stunned. This was the last thing I expected her to say or do. "What? You do know that it takes time for the donor to recover? That's if you're a match. And you've got to be ready to jump on the first plane out of here as soon as the movie's called. How's all that going to work?"

Having her stay home forever might be the bonus I had longed for, but I didn't want it to happen this way. Not because of her wanting to do good in the world. Star had so much to offer. She was so freakin' talented it scared me at times. Watching her sing or dance often left me in wonder. The world needed her more than our mother who'd abandoned her all those years ago did.

"I don't know. I just don't want her to die. I mean, she just got back to town. Maybe she's changed? We could have loads of time together yet. People with a donated kidney can live for years."

Anger at thoughts of a scalpel being taken to my beautiful sister came boiling to the surface. "You don't know that! Maybe she's just going to wreck a new kidney too and you'll live your whole life with only one. And say you have a problem later on, and you need both of them. No, I won't let you do it!"

"You can't stop me! You're not the boss of me."

I shook my head, my mind made up. "No. If someone has to do this thing, it won't be you."

"Who then? Tulip's petrified of needles and blood, and you won't do it. You still blame her for *everything*."

"Who else am I supposed to blame? No one put a gun to her head and told her to abandon us or take drugs, did they? It was all her doing. If it weren't for Granny, we'd be long dead. Frozen to death in a snowbank somewhere. You think about that when you see her."

"She was sick. Hooked on the drugs. Blame the distributors if you need someone to blame. Or her genetics. But I'm going to be checked out—see if we're a match. And if we are, I'm going ahead with it. The movie people can wait. If they want me bad enough, they will." I saw what the words cost, her throat working as she swallowed over a lump. I had one too, aching like mad. Tears were threatening to fall.

"Let me check you out. See how your health is."

"Not necessary." She pulled her hands away and stood up.

"Please, I need to know."

"You can check me out if we're a match."

"Why bother to find out if you're a match if your body's not up to the operation?" I pushed at her, wanting answers. *Now.*

"You'll say anything to stop me and I'm fine. Healthy as the proverbial horse. End of discussion. Now go get ready. I'll stay and work in the café today. Someone needs to hold down the fort while you're gone. *Again.*"

The poke slid right off me, my worry for her wellbeing too high to let such a small matter upset me. Suddenly I wanted to see her cheeky robot dance in the worst way.

"Promise me you won't do anything rash? Please."

"Well, it's not like they can operate today. It takes weeks and weeks between testing and scheduling and everything else that goes into it." She didn't look me in the eye as she recited the words.

"How do you know all that? Have you talked to Doc Tanner already?"

She flushed to the roots of her fair hair. "Yeah, okay, I've been asking questions. Not like you got the time right now. I'll bet you didn't spend all day yesterday thinking about it and worrying. Probably too busy trying to be a superhero."

That stung. And she was right. I had done everything in my power to avoid thinking on the subject that she had obviously dwelled on all day.

"I wasn't given my gifts just to waste them anymore than you were. I don't want you doing this. You'll need time to heal. And knowing the convergence of energy in the universe, it will all happen just as you've been called to do the movie. So, I've come to a decision."

I took a deep breath. Could I really do it? *Yes.* To protect Star, I could. I had to get it to before I thought any more because a wave of fear also struck that I struggled with. This was such a big thing, who knew how my body would react?

"I'll be the donor. I'm the one with the universal blood type O, so likely I'll be a match for whatever else they throw at me. And I'm the one who never gets sick. Remember the bad bouts with flu and cold you and Tulip get every winter while I get off scot-free? And I've got plenty of helpers to allow me time to recover, between the coven and people looking for work. So yeah, I can do this."

Star stared at me, her eyes liquid with unshed tears. "You don't have to decide this right now. We can talk about it more."

"No talking. I'll do it if everyone just *stops* talking about it."

"Do what?" We'd both missed Tulip coming in the backdoor.

I groaned, but before I could say anything, Star got right to the point. "We're talking about mom and her needing a kidney. I wanted to do it, but Charm's stepping up."

"No!" Tulip surprised both of us by vehemently whipping her head back and forth. "I don't want either of you taking that chance. I was reading about infections and other problems associated with the operation."

"I'm young and beyond healthy, sis. It will be a breeze for me. So, don't worry, *and please*, no more discussion on this subject. We'll just get to it when it's time. Now, I've got a ton of things to do today. Star, could you bring her up to speed on what I'm off to do? I gotta get going. I'm running late as it is."

Chapter Seventeen

A few minutes later, I had a sleeping bag guaranteed to sub-zero temperatures tied to a backpack with proper supplies to make it through a chilly night on the barren landscape. I tossed the items onto the passenger seat of my Jeep, started up Thor's engine and prayed I could slip out of town unnoticed. I drove slowly down the alley, keeping a sharp lookout, then crossed the street and continued down the next alley to avoid Main Street until I was on the edge of town. Turning south on Telegraph Road, I continued toward the highway, not breathing easily until I was about a mile out of town, headed west toward Gold Mountain.

Ah, the trees were in full glory, golds and reds that brought a twinge of sadness to my soul. *Such ephemeral beauty. Well, most beauty is transient, Charm*, I reminded myself. The wheel of the year constantly turned. I pushed my thoughts away from the changes that were coming, no matter how I felt about them, and instead focused on the investigation. I was excited about what revelations today might bring that my foot pressed harder on the gas pedal as the town vanished in the rearview mirror. I wanted to get there already.

It wasn't far to drive, just over an hour, but the hike that loomed was daunting. I parked Thor in a sheltered area at the edge of a copse of willows and loaded the backpack with the sleeping bag onto my shoulders. Even including only bare essentials, it was a load that would grow heavier by the hour. I debated, chewing on my bottom lip. Was it better to go lighter and hope to get out before dark or better to be prepared? I heard Ace's voice in my head, saying about what I would expect. *If you're going to be a fool, darlin', at least be a safe one.*

"Well, wish me luck, Thor."

I patted his hood, the red paint flaking off in my hand. If only I could afford a new paint job. Maybe soon with the way internet sales were picking up, a slightly bigger trickle each week. I donned my aviator sunglasses and began my trek. The secret would be staying hydrated, and that was the reason for the heavy load. Sure, there was water in the tributaries that ran down from Gold Mountain, but the water quality I could not speak to. I far preferred lugging my own fresh supply.

Two hours into the hike, I stopped to catch a breath and drink some of that precious water. I'd neglected breakfast and dug out an energy bar to compensate. An eagle soared against the robin's-egg-blue sky when I looked upward, its spirit lifting mine while blessing my adventure. I'd been making good headway so far, following trails between rocks that were increasing in size the closer I got to my destination while staying clear of cold streams of shallow water in efforts to keep my feet dry. My mind had locked in the treasure map and I brought it up now to check my bearings. I overlaid the map in my mind on the physical landscape, an ability that allowed me to easily check my sightlines. *Yup. Right on target.*

I recapped the water bottle then got up from the stump I had rested on. At this pace, I just might make it out before dark. Two more hours later and the straps were digging and chafing the tops of my shoulder blades. I shifted the load to try to find a spot that didn't hurt. *Reminder to self – hike with a pack more often.* I was a bit more out of shape than I had realized, taking my perfect constitution for granted.

Finishing my first bottle of water, I was grateful the load would now be a bit lighter. It was early afternoon, according to my cellphone that held, surprisingly, no bars of reception. *Phttt.* The angle of the sun was more useful. It was October in the far north, which meant that sunset was not many hours away. The thought made me increase my pace, though the rocks were growing larger and the debris strewn on the path more challenging.

I checked the sightlines again when the sun had begun its short angle of descent toward the horizon, resigned to staying out overnight. Well, I had bear spray, a taser and cold food to keep from alerting hostile creatures. Snug in my sleeping bag, I would stay warm at least. Now sleeping? That might be a bit challenging, unless I could find a safe place to sleep. Up a tree would make me happiest, but our trees weren't the trees of southern regions with their wider stances.

I wasn't far from that big red X now. My mind kept itself occupied, overlaying the landscape to check the location every few minutes. It sure beat dwelling on today's conversation with Star. *Later*, I promised myself.

With an hour and a half of daylight left, the sky began to turn gunmetal gray in a ridiculous hurry, the clouds rushing in from the west where most of the Canadian weather originated, swooping down from the Rockies and gathering speed over the prairies. *Great.* Now it was imperative I found a decent spot to spend the night — at the very least the temperature would drop.

When I finally struggled over the last of the trail, somehow avoiding breaking an ankle or two, and skirting around the final boulder, I found a small outcropping of stone with some dead trees standing guard. Twenty feet farther on would be the X indicated on the treasure map. But the trees were a tangled mess of limbs and branches and stood right in my way like the knurliest fence ever.

I sighed and moved forward. The brambles tore at my clothing and backpack mercilessly as I tried to push my way through. If nothing else, they'd be a good guard against any animal attack. And low and behold, a small cave opening greeted me after an immense struggle. *No. Just no.* I disliked Skull Cave, but this one was far smaller and about gave me a heart-quake.

This was the spot, whether I liked it or not. I could see why it was believed to be haunted with all those gnarly trees guarding a creepy cave. Freakin' scary as Hades and guaranteed to knock a few years off anyone's life. *Okay, grow a pair, Charm.*

I slipped off my backpack, found my hardhat with the handy-dandy light attached, got on my hands and knees and wormed my way inside the entrance. A few feet later the opening increased, and just ahead, I could see with the help of the battery-powered light a larger space. I was grateful to be able to stand up in the cavern about the size of my apartment back home, a place I wished I was at that moment, reading a well-thumbed, well-loved Agatha Christie novel and drinking a glass of refreshing white wine spritzer with a slice of orange. *No dice.* I was standing, dusty and sweaty, inside a mine that was reputed to be haunted. At least I'd have tales for my grandchildren…if I lived to see them.

The walls were rough-hewn, with indications of pickaxes having been used sometime in the past to increase the space, and I turned my attention to checking it out. *Aha.* Bits of color were noticeable in the rockface, running in shallow veins around the ancient room. There was gold for the having, if one were willing to work hard for it.

Why had it been abandoned? I laid my hand against the wall, trying to feel its energy. Someone had been here! Quite recently in fact. So, the place wasn't abandoned at all. The difficult structures outside had been left on purpose to make it harder to locate. Most people wouldn't have bothered coming inside here. Well, it would be my place to sleep tonight.

But first, I would walk the entire area, keeping an eye out for any traces of animal scat. I stumbled a few seconds later, my foot connecting with something. *A skull.* I swore it leered at me in the dimness, its empty eye sockets illuminated by my head lamp.

Oh, my goddess. Another shock to my system. The skull was accompanied by long bones, and it was most definitely the skull of a human being. A former human being, to be precise. This had to be the ghost of Gold Mountain, and there was no way in Hades I was spending the night in the cave with a skeleton. And whose skeleton exactly? No one was missing in town. It must have been really old, from decades earlier. Had there been a disagreement about gold? Someone who had come upon this cave, then got ill and died of natural causes?

I didn't know. But I wasn't touching the bones again to discover anything more. I made an about-face and rejoined the outside world as fast as my body could wiggle itself through the confines of the tunnel. Filled with regret that it was now too dark to head home, I decided, albeit reluctantly, that it would be best to set up camp right there behind the barrier of trees and in front of the cave. Scary, but a broken leg in the pitch dark was even scarier.

The caw of a murder of crows made the hair stand up all over my body. Where was my lucky eagle spirit animal when I needed one? I struggled to get my mind under control, then hunkered down to make a campsite that would at least make me feel productive.

It was also easier to stay put then try to make my way through the barrier of trees when they were such a great shield against stray predators. But the yawning mouth of the cave, with the deceased inside, was daunting. Maybe I should pull all the extra bushes and rocks I could procure over the entrance? I set to work, filling the gap with some success. I sat back on my haunches. At least now I'd have some warning if anything untoward occurred. Though what stunts a dead guy could pull I didn't know.

I laid out my bedroll with my head away from the cave's entrance, as far as I could manage. Tomorrow I would be reporting the situation, but right now, I just wanted to keep my mind off what had happened long ago in the depths of that cave.

I decided against lighting a fire, as much as I longed for one, being too worried about the dry dead trees catching fire, and set about having a meal. *Cold.* But decent enough to keep body and soul together.

A hoot owl called in the darkness and I swallowed. An owl was an agent known to herald death. Not fond of such omens, I wanted to hear the reassuring screech of an eagle or two.

I sat bundled up in the sleeping bag after a supper that consisted of a ham sandwich and an apple, my ears alert for any noise. So far it had not rained or snowed, but the sky was starless, meaning a thick layer of clouds had moved in. I had a blue plastic tarp fixed over my head just in case, held up by a tripod of tree limbs. I was cozy and warm, but my accelerated heart rate suggested otherwise. Every few seconds, I glanced involuntarily toward the mouth of the cave. I couldn't imagine sleeping anytime soon. It was going to be the longest night of my life if I couldn't make peace with the skeleton in the cave. Maybe I should have dared the path home…

A couple of hours dragged by, second by second. My eyes darted around like a couple of out-of-control ping pong balls. Then suddenly a weird light made itself known. It shone through the bushes in wavering circles, kind of about what one would expect from an alien spacecraft. I wiggled out of my cocoon in double-time. I'd never go down without a fight. *Family pride thing.*

"Charm? Charm McCall?" a voice called from the distance. *Thank goodness. A voice I recognize.*

"I'm over here, behind all the trees and bushes."

I stood and watched my very own Mr. Bigfoot struggle to get his massive body through the same well-protected bramble nature fence that I had endured. It took enough time that I had not one fingernail left unbitten before he emerged.

He stood before me, my sturdy Mountie dressed in hiking gear with a pack similar to mine on his back. His expression was so inscrutable that I tensed up even more.

"Evening, Ace."

"Miss McCall."

"How did you find me?"

"Did you really think I was going to fall for your spending the entire day in a beauty salon? A gal who looks like you?"

"What? You don't think I look good?" I think my jaw might have hit the ground. I spit out a bug that had made its way unimpeded inside my mouth.

"Darlin', you look so good every day that was no way you needed a minute at a spa, let along an entire day."

"Huh." *Brilliant.* Shocked into silence, I waited to see what would happen next.

"Would you mind telling me what you're doing out here? Why you are not at home safe and sound in your bed? And why you didn't tell me about this little sojourn of yours?"

"I didn't want to worry you. Besides, you're needed in town. You got an important investigation to conduct." My excuse sounded lame spoken in the dark and subject to Ace's scrutiny. It was time to be completely honest. "I wanted some time alone to think. You know, with all that's happening with my mother?"

"Ah, I see." I could see my answer surprised him. "I'm sorry for interrupting, then."

"Don't be. I'm a little spooked. And I'm sorry if I worried you. Can we be done with that part now and move on? I found a skeleton in the cave that I've been keeping an eye on."

"Sure, but first I want to say I'm glad to find you all right. And I do understand your need to be by yourself to think things through. I came because I was worried. A woman alone where wild animals roam free? Not a good scenario."

I swallowed. "Thanks for checking up on me. It was a bit spookier than I expected."

"You're welcome. I'm thinking we should stay put until morning. Check on the skeleton then. You okay with staying overnight?"

"Yes." *More than okay.* Now I could sleep. *Well, maybe?* With a hunk like Ace so close by, that would present its own unique set of challenges.

He began to remove his backpack then set to blowing up an air mattress with a portable handheld device. Soon his bed looked far more comfortable than mine…and just a few feet away from mine, closer to the cave entrance. *Perfect.*

"You do come well prepared."

"I had no idea what condition I'd find you in. I brought a first-aid kit and a satellite phone to call for help if need be."

Those words struck me hard. Well, more the tone really, as though I'd had worried him more than he wanted to say.

"Ace, I really am sorry. It's just been weird lately and I needed to get away."

"Thank you. And I do understand. Maybe I shouldn't have come. But I was worried about you all alone out here."

"I need a hug." The raw words hung between us.

He turned from laying out the covers on the mattress and we faced each other. Then I stepped forward into his welcoming arms. *Oh my.* His heat warmed me through and through, a lifeline in a violent storm.

We held each other for a few minutes in silence, his chin resting on the top of my head.

"You smell so good," Ace said. Our hearts were beating in tandem, his chest rising against my body as he took deep breaths. "Like wildflowers on a summer's breeze."

My heart truly melted and love moved in deeper, filling all the empty spaces that my life had created over the years, all the painful places my childhood had caused. I felt whole. Renewed. And I took a few satisfying breaths of my own, bringing his essence into the depths of my soul.

Chapter Eighteen

Ace pulled away first and I was grateful. There was no point in taking unnecessary chances.

"So, maybe I should have a bit of food then turn in." His voice sounded a little strangled and I knew he was experiencing the same rush of libido.

"Sounds good. What did you bring with you?"

"I packed in a hurry, so just some protein bars and energy drinks."

"Sorry about that. I'll make it up to you by cooking a special supper for you soon as we get home."

"I think I should be offered a series of those fabulous meals of yours. I did hike through hours of rough terrain today."

"Don't press your luck, Constable. So, did you learn anything today before you headed off after me?"

"I didn't have that much time before I discovered your ruse. But tomorrow I hope to glean a bit more of the truth. It's quite the fascinating puzzle."

"Yeah, I think even our beloved Agatha Christie would have her work cut out for her." I sat cross-legged on my sleeping roll and watched Ace rummage around in his backpack.

He sat on his air mattress, the foil on the bar rustling as he tore it open and bit into it. He munched in silence and I waited for him to eat a couple of the bars then gulp down an energy drink, followed by a small bottle of water.

"Better?" I asked.

"Beats nothing." He tucked the garbage created by his meal into a reusable bag and slid it into his bag. He removed his hat and lay it on top of the pile before unlacing his boots and tugging them off. Such homey actions stirred me. This was a first for me, spending time on a camping trip with a man—exhilarating and scary. But I was grateful to feel ever so much safer, just in case a ghost decided to give us a show. Considering the events of this past year—so many changes—I wouldn't rule it out.

Ace left his clothes on and slid under the wool covering before tucking it neatly all around his huge body. I did the same, enjoying the sensation of being so close to him in the darkness, freeing and intimate, at the same time.

"I tried to heal my mom today." Just saying it out loud was cathartic. Maybe he was right that I needed to talk about this more.

"That must have been a hard thing for you." He said the words without judgment. It was times like this, when I was with Ace, that I wanted to be a better person. *Rise above the petty.* Was I being too hard on my mom? Maybe I did need to talk to her soon, make some peace with our checkered past and not just sweep everything under the rug.

"It was. She's really sick and I can't heal her entirely, just buy her some time. And Star said she wanted to be her kidney donor."

"Star? Huh."

I pressed on, my stomach suddenly in knots, my breathing too rapid. "But I told her no way she can be doing that, especially right now with all her plans. So," I took a deep breath. "I said I'd do it."

A heavy silence greeted my pronouncement.

"That's a hard thing to hear." He cleared his throat, his tone huskier. "I can't say it makes me happy to think about what you would have to go through, physically and emotionally. But it does fit who you are, always protecting your family. I'll stand by you every step of the way."

"Thanks. That means a lot to me." *More than I can say.*

I pulled the covers up to my chin. "Good night, Ace."

"Night, darlin'."

I thought sleep would come immediately, as it usually did for me after long days on my feet in the café, but as I lay there in the darkness, the wonderful sounds of Ace's rhythmic breaths tantalizing the air, I found myself wide awake. My twenty-first year had brought so many changes, and one of the best was the man who slept so soundly at my side.

But then I must have slept, because the next thing, my eyes were opening to find the darkness gone. Ace was already awake, pulling on his boots.

"Mornin' darlin'."

"Morning, Ace." I stretched and threw off my cover.

"How did you sleep?"

"I feel great. Slept like a rock. You?"

"Same. It's the country air." He smiled at me before continuing to lace up his boots.

I got up and scrambled for my own hiking boots, pulling them on and tying them in place. Homey things and packing up our belongings continued to keep us both occupied for a few minutes.

"Guess there's no ghost of Gold Mountain. Or at least I didn't get a visit last night. You?" Ace asked, his mouth lifted in a small smile as he munched on another protein bar.

"No." I shook my head. "That's more baby Ling Ling's territory."

His eyebrows shot up. "If you say so. But I'll tell you, I'm really missing my coffee this morning."

"Me too. I owe you a pot as soon as we get home." I gave him my cutie-pie contrite look. After all, it was my doing that he was out in the wilderness in the first place. At least it hadn't rained or snowed. That would have really sucked.

"You're on. Okay, time to see about that skeleton."

I shivered. "Yeah, guess so." I went over to the opening and began to yank away all the debris I had tried to fill the entrance way with. I snorted. As if ghosts couldn't slip through brambles. What had I been thinking last night?

"That is one small opening," Ace remarked, obviously pondering the situation. He was much larger-framed, larger-than-life than any other man in Snowy Lake, an added bonus in just about any situation except the one currently facing us.

"I had to wiggle to get through it and there's no other way in. A regular-sized man could get through, but you might want to rethink going inside. Perhaps I should just go in and collect the bones? Not much to see in there, unless you are a gold miner. A lot of gold still there."

I put on my brave face. It really wasn't that hard with a big strong Mountie at my side. It was just that I didn't feel really comfortable around bones that weren't properly blessed and buried. I blessed all our food every time I cooked or baked. And these bones had belonged to someone. Well, at least that someone would now be properly buried. I'd see to it personally. *And a headstone erected.*

"I might have to take you up on your suggestion. Or we leave it as it is and come back with equipment to increase the size of the hole. Are you sure there was nothing other than the bones?"

"Just the bones. Kind of tossed into a pile, so I'm not sure what could be learned anyway. The crime scene is so old now, if it *is* a crime scene? Maybe someone just crawled in there to die?" The thought made my skin itch.

"I think we should take them with us. I don't want them disappearing, if they're evidence."

"Oh, I forgot— I sensed that someone had been in there not that long ago."

"That decides it. We take them with us."

Great. Just the outcome I didn't like to contemplate. I took a deep breath. *Best to get it over with.* "What shall I put them in?"

I yanked on my hardhat while Ace went to his backpack and pulled out a large white plastic bag. "This'll work. Oh, and take photos too, before you move them."

He handed the bag to me and I dutifully thrust it into my jeans pocket. "Okay, I'm off then." I grimaced a smile and crouched down, getting onto my knees to push myself into the entranceway. I made a production of wiggling myself in and heard a chuckle of laughter from Ace. That helped, and I hurried to get to the point where I could stand upright again.

The bones lay where I had left them, gleaming whitely in the light that slanted down from my hardhat. I took a series of overlapping photos on my phone, then tugged on my gloves and got down on my haunches. Giving a silent prayer to the goddess that I meant no harm, I began to carefully place them in the bag. It went well at first, with me blessing each bone before gingerly picking them up and slipping them out of sight in the growing packet or remains.

But when I picked up the skull, it happened. *An instantaneous vision.* He had been working right here, digging for gold with his sweat and tears. And he had paid in blood as well. Someone hit him from behind and he was falling. Falling. Then he knew no more. Oh, how I wished he could have shown me who had done the foul deed, because justice must happen, no matter that the murder had happened decades ago. I would personally see to it.

When no bones remained, I got to my feet and said a final sacred prayer. Then I reversed my process out of the cave, bringing the bones into the sunlight for the first time in years.

I handed the bag over to Ace. "The guy was murdered. Hit from behind."

"You learned that from touching the bones?'

I nodded. "They spoke to me. There's proof on the back of the skull that confirms it." I pointed at the package where the damage was clearly visible.

"An old murder." The way he just took my word for it made it seem all-the-more normal to know these things.

"Yes. There could be a tie-in to the recent ones. Oh, by the way, I was able to pretty much eliminate Josie as a suspect. I took a reading and didn't find anything that implicated her, though I discovered she has a brilliant mind."

"So do you."

I blushed under the compliment. We were really beginning to mesh as cohorts in investigations and it felt darn good.

"Thanks."

"I've been able to pretty much eliminate Josie as well. There's no connection between her and the second victim. And those two were murdered by the same person or persons."

"Eric and Floyd are still front and center. Have you discovered any connections there?"

"There's the bowling alley connection. And Eric was also seen talking to the second victim later that same night. Plus, a friend went with Eric to visit Sergei that morning, Buddy Harrison. He wasn't listed in the ledger, because he didn't buy anything. Just went along for the ride."

"I didn't know that." I didn't know Buddy well, but Auntie T.J. did. I'd get her take on him and check him out.

"See? It's good to share information."

"Yeah. I hear you." I nodded.

"Unfortunately, your aunt doesn't see things that way." As we talked, Ace went about storing the bones carefully in his backpack.

I gave an exaggerated sigh. *You can't pick your relatives.* Then I felt bad. I loved her, even if she could be a real pain in the hiney. "She's still not coming clean?"

"No. I need you to stress to her the importance of making a full confession when we get back to town. I need to know what she's hiding."

"Oh, let me tell you, I'm ready to force a confession out of her if I have to tie her to a chair and feed her my special truth serum."

Ace startled, turning his brown eyes my way and locking me in his sights. "You can do that? You have such an item in your arsenal?"

It would have been so much fun to just go along with it, but I didn't want to upset the lovely goodwill we had achieved. "No. I can't. Besides, it would be unethical. But I can bribe her." I grinned. "She's very fond of being in her sister's good books. And if all else fails, I'll corral her and take a reading. She can't hide the truth from me much longer. And I think the goddess will forgive me in the investigation of a crime. At least I hope so."

"When it's for a higher cause and you do no harm, I think most things are forgivable to any higher entity that one worships."

"Remember that next time, eh!"

His eyebrows knitted together, the intensity in his eyes instantly turning cooler. "Miss McCall, we've discussed this already. I have your word that you won't do such things again without consulting me. As my dad always said — and I'm in full agreement with him — if you're humble enough and smart enough, you'll learn something from every decision."

"Right." I deflated. Why is it that others cannot see the importance of allowing a spirit to be free? I know my limits. I don't need to be reminded of them at every twist and turn.

Chapter Nineteen

It was a long, long trek back to town. Ace wouldn't use his special RCMP phone to have someone come to our aid. As he pointed out, there was no actual emergency. My aching muscles didn't quite agree, but I held my mouth clamped shut, knowing I had brought this on myself.

But I was going to begin a workout routine when I got back home. I took a full-fledged vow right there, stomping down the trail, sweat dripping into my eyes. The day had turned out to be warmer with clear skies. And when Thor finally came into view, I could have kissed the very ground he was parked on.

"Okay, I'll see you back in town." I made a rush for my Jeep. Well, more like I stumbled over to it, right out of a jam.

"I'll follow you." Ace gave me *the look*—the one suggesting he had me in his sights and was keeping it that way.

"I already said I was going to behave. What more do you want?" I mumbled to myself as I got into the driver's seat, putting the key into its slot and turning over the motor. Nothing. I tried again. Silence. The motor was dead. *No.* I groaned and laid my head on the steering wheel. *Shoot. I'm sorry, Thor. I should have checked your battery before we left town.*

I waited a full minute, sent a prayer, then tried again. *No dice.* I picked up my backpack and trudged over to the SUV. Ace was on the phone, his expression dead serious. *Now what?*

"Your aunt's up and left town," he said without any preamble.

My heart sank. "Why on earth would she do that? Now, of all times. She promised to look after my mother—"

Ace's expression shifted, sympathy turning his brown eyes to pools of liquid. I averted my eyes and pressed my lips together.

"Apparently"—he cleared his throat—"Star's seeing to your mother. At least she was there when Winn Duffy dropped by the house to ask your aunt a couple of questions yesterday afternoon. You know, since I wasn't there, he filled in."

"Now you're blaming me? I didn't ask you to come after me! I was doing just fine on my own." I would have walked away, but I had no other choice for a ride home and I needed to get there urgently to see what the heck was going on.

"No blame." He sighed. "Just stating facts. I'm sorry I brought up your mother. I know you're going through a difficult time."

"No one can know what it's like, except maybe Star and Tulip, how I really feel about it." I heard the petulance in my tone and straightened up. No good came of being childish, that much I was learning.

"Of course not. I was just meaning you have a lot on your plate right now, and I don't want to add to it."

Why does he have to be such a great guy? "Sorry, just hearing that Auntie has disappeared, it—"

"I know you're not comfortable talking about your mother, but if there's anything I can do?" He looked so sweet and helpful, I wanted to just crawl into his arms and forget about the upcoming trauma that would certainly be visited on my family over my mother needing a kidney. *Mine.*

"Thanks. I'm working on it settling things in mind." I grimaced. "Looks like I need a ride back to town. My Jeep won't start. Battery's dead."

His glance flitted to Thor. "No problem. We'll have your ride towed and seen to. I'll make the call right now."

I left him to the call, threw my things in the back seat and climbed in the passenger side of the police vehicle. I settled back, staring blankly at the horizon while my mind mulled over things. Why had my auntie taken off? Had she been involved in the death of Sergei? The thought made my stomach churn with unease. *Maybe it was an accident? Something happened that she didn't want to admit to?* What was in the darn moonshine anyway? That was obviously a key. If only we had the toxicology results back.

Ace got in behind the wheel and turned to me. "Tug's sending someone from town to pick up your Jeep."

"Thanks. How soon until we get those toxicology results? Any idea?"

"Soon, I hope. Maybe by the weekend, if not, next week. These things take time, unfortunately."

I sat and watched the nearly uninhabited landscape zip by the window with no traffic headed our way, wishing it WERE me driving the souped-up police vehicle. *Must have at least three hundred and fifty freakin' horsepower under that hood.* I'd have the siren on full blast, pedal to the metal, and be in town before I could say "Auntie T.J.'s getting a kick where the sun don't shine".

"Doesn't this thing *go* any faster?" Pushing my foot down on the floorboards wasn't accomplishing anything, except to annoy me further when the vehicle did not respond. I had certainly picked the wrong day to leave town. I could have talked my auntie out of doing something so foolish as to take off. And where were my sisters in all this?

Ace's mouth twitched. "What's the rush? I thought we were enjoying each other's company?"

I gave an eyeroll. "We can see each other *anytime*. I'll even chip in for gas if you'll push it harder."

"You do have a hard time following the rules." He shook his head. "Better to arrive in one piece than not to arrive at all."

He did step it up a bit though and the speedometer climbed a few satisfying degrees. If only I knew a spell to make an engine stroke its pistons quicker. *Not enough practical spells in the grimoires*, in my personal opinion.

"What's your take on us getting away for a few days after this investigation is concluded?"

"Say what?" His question was right out of left field.

"I was thinking I have a few days of holiday banked, what with all the overtime I've been putting in, so maybe we could go to Winnipeg? Spend some time with my parents and see some of the sights? Stay at the famous Fort Garry Hotel. You could even have a real spa day at their facilities. What do you say, darlin'? You up for a bit of adventure?"

"Ah, maybe. Hard to think that far ahead with everything going on."

"Well, just think about it. No rush on answering. When the case is solved and things are settled with your mother, we can talk about it then."

"Ah, *when the case is solved*. Those are good words." At least I hoped they were, praying my auntie was not in this neck-deep. *Because that would be a game changer.* But no, it couldn't be that. There had to be some logical explanation.

I took a deep breath. "Thanks for being there. I know I'm a bit touchy about my family."

He turned those devastatingly melting chocolate brown eyes my way, the look lighting the usual fire in my soul. *And parts farther south.* "You know how I feel about you. You brighten up my life. I'd just like the chance to get away from here and spend some alone time with you. You know, when we're not just solving cases?"

"I hear you. Me too. When the case is concluded and things with my mother are settled, we'll go away for a few days."

"Sounds good. I'll hold you to that."

I was grateful he didn't reopen the discussion about donating a kidney. I didn't want to talk about it anymore, just do it and move on. It was the best thing for it.

Ace slowed down as the outskirts of town came into view and the posted legal speed reduced to town speed. The past hour had flown by. I savored what felt like a better footing in our two-steps-forward-and-one back relationship. Bonus, we had a mini-vacation planned. Now, a quick resolution to the murders and we'd be home free.

"You coming in? I got a full pot of coffee with your name on it and a country-style breakfast special that will top you up." I held the passenger door open and spoke at him through the opening.

"Much as I would love that, I'd better get home, shower and head over to the detachment." He looked resigned and apologetic.

"Still got to eat, don't you? Come by when you're free and I'll see to it personally."

"Now that's an invitation a man can't resist. See you as soon as I can get away."

I scurried into the café to be met by the sight of Granny and my sisters huddled around a booth.

"We were all worried about you, sweeting." Granny Toogood's mild rebuke was almost more than I could bear. Nothing bothered me more than giving her a minute's worry.

"I'm sorry I worried you. It wasn't my intention. I just had to get to the bottom of the mystery of why Gold Mountain was connected. Besides, I had company last night, so I wasn't all alone to face any danger that came my way."

"It was good that Constable Collins headed off after you." She nodded.

"Did you discover anything important?" Tulip asked.

"I did, but before I share, I'm desperate for coffee." I got up and poured a mugful of the priceless substance. I also grabbed a quiche from the display case and settled back into the booth.

"Did Auntie T.J. leave any word?" I asked, gulping coffee and munching on my breakfast, finishing both in record time.

"Yeah, make of it as you will. Quote, '*when you're up to your hiney in alligators, time to throw the chum.*'"

"Sounds like Auntie T.J. So helpful."

"Do you think she had anything to do with all this?" Star asked. I checked her out, and she was looking better today. "I mean, leaving town right now? It doesn't look good. People are talking."

"Just ignore it. I'm sure we'll hear something soon. It's not like it's the first time she's up and done this. By the way, who's looking after Mom? I thought Ace mentioned you had gone over there, Star?" I finished my coffee and got up to pour another mugful.

"I got Christine to fill in for me this morning."

"Yeah, Auntie T.J. takes after our mother. Or I should say, Mom takes after her." Tulip's tone held a trace of bitterness.

"Now, recriminations don't help. Tell us about your journey, sweeting."

I told the tale, including finding the skeleton and ending with Ace's invitation.

"We'll see to having the bones buried properly, of course," Granny spoke up right away.

"I think it's important." I nodded.

"Nice about Ace's vacation idea. You two should get away. You never take a day off from work or helping our town." Tulip looked happy for me.

"But you promised to give Mom a kidney." Star looked less excited.

"One doesn't negate the other. I'm still going ahead with it, as soon as it can be arranged. I'll take a few days for the vacation as recovery time."

Granny Toogood shook her head. "It will take more than a few days to recover, even though your instincts are the finest. I'd say we'd better all step up our game and make sure your sister gets lots of rest afterward."

There were nods all around, except for Tulip, who looked like she was supressing something. *What is the deal with her?*

But I was pleased Granny wasn't questioning my decision. I didn't want to fight with anyone in my family or discuss it further.

I glanced at the busily ticking clock over the coffee area, a dead ringer for our rooster clock in the kitchen. "Now, I have to shower and clean up. Ace may be coming by for breakfast."

"So, tell me, how far did you two get last night?" Star dogged my footsteps all the way to the kitchen. "I mean, you two, all alone in the wilderness with sleeping bags? I've watched you guys. You're smoking hot when you're together. Couldn't be a more perfect time to grab some, eh!"

"Nothing happened, Miss Smarty Pants. It was all business. Plus, we were guarding a murder site, which takes the romance out of the equation." I heard the prissiness in my tone.

"Yeah, right! You were guarding a dead guy. Not much competition there." Her eyes held a smugness that grated. "I know you can't talk in front of Granny, but you can tell me, sis. *Anything.*"

"It's complicated, okay? Now, I gotta shower."

"Go right ahead. Nothing stopping you." As happy as I was to see Star was reverting to her old self, a part of me wished for a longer break from her manic glee. Not that I ever wanted to see her as sad as she'd been yesterday morning ever again as long as I lived.

I raced upstairs, hurrying to prepare for the day. The pressure was on. With Auntie gone from the scene, I needed to wrap this case up ASAP to take all the focus off her. *Please, oh please, don't let her have had anything to do with it.*

Chapter Twenty

Two hours later, and still no Ace. I'd caught up in all the orders for spells in the in-basket for Saturday night's event, served customers and had even found out the name associated with baby Ling Ling's ghost. She'd spelled out the word *gold* and *bones*, possibly meaning the skeleton from the cave, but how she'd seen him in town was anyone's guess. Didn't ghosts usually favor the place they'd died?

"Winn Duffy must have got on his case and sent him right back to work." I said, remembering I also wanted to check out Buddy Harrison, Eric's friend. "I need to get out of here. I have a lead to check out. Can you mind the store, Tulip?"

"Huh? Oh yeah, sure, whatever." Tulip was lost in her own world this morning, glued to her computer screen. I'd guess it was her way of coping.

I sighed.

"You know you're not the only person in our family who can be a hero."

Her words stunned me and I hesitated with my hand on the doorknob. "What do you mean?"

Her chin wobbled and her blue eyes filled with tears. "I mean, why didn't someone think of me? I'm just the middle triplet, ignored and left to my own devices while Star's the center of attention and you — well, you're Charm McCall, with enough gifts to choke a horse."

"I'm sorry. I didn't know you felt that way. I thought you were scared of blood and hospitals?"

"I am, but it doesn't mean I can't step up. Do the right thing." She shook her head angrily, swiping at the tears. "I don't want anything to happen to you. I mean, you're my sis-sis...ter." A sob punctuated her words.

I went to put my arms around her. "Hush. Everything's going to be okay, sweeting." I found myself using Granny's term for us.

Her body quaked a couple of times, then she settled down. "You promise everything's going to be okay?"

"I'm sure everything's going to be just fine. We'll all sail through this and it will be just a memory in a year's time." I wasn't quite as certain of my words as I would like to have been, but I wasn't letting on to her. *Yeah, sure, I'm scared. It's a big deal at twenty-one to think of such a big operation.* I just had to pray things would work out. *There are no coincidences, right?* It meant that this journey had been long-planned, as hard as it was for all of us. I had to believe that, needed to see myself coming out the other side unscathed.

"Okay. Sorry I was such a pill." Tulip straightened and gave me a small smile.

"No problem, sis. If you're okay, I've got to try and get some information off a suspect?"

"Sure, I'll hold down the fort. See you later."

I double-timed it down the street. Buddy Harrison worked at Tug's Tire shop, and if I hurried, I could catch him before he went to lunch.

An impact gun, with its *tat-a-tat* cacophony of deafening sounds, echoed deep inside the shadowy depths of the garage. The distinct odor of burned rubber and old oil assaulted my nostrils. The ear-piercing sounds abruptly stopped when Buddy Harrison caught sight of me walking toward him.

He frowned and stepped back from tightening the bolts on the front tire on a navy-blue Buick sedan that I recognized as belonging to an elderly couple in town who never drove it above five-miles-an-hour and on Sundays only. The tire had most likely gone flat out of boredom.

"Charm McCall." Then his expression cleared. "You've come about your Jeep. It's not here yet. Tug just left to pick it up. Short-handed today. Dale's out with a flu bug."

"No problem. Actually, I wanted to speak with you."

"Yeah, that so?" He pursed his lips and folded his arms over his broad chest and belly, his body type pretty much interchangeable with most middle-aged men in our town.

"It's come to my attention that you were with Eric on Saturday night. At the Bowl-a-ram-a?"

"What of it? I already discussed it with your Mountie friend."

I ignored the supposed dig.

"It's no secret that Eric and I hang out. That we meet a new guy in town. Not my fault he ups and gets himself killed straight off. Seemed like an okay guy."

He shrugged. "Didn't have much time to get to know him, if you know what I mean."

"Yes, sad state of affairs. What did you guys talk about?"

"Not much of anything, really." He looked away as he said it, his eyes twitching. Right. *You discussed something you're desperate to hide.*

"Why was Jon Rail in town? Do you know that at least?"

"Looking for work, I think." He grimaced. "Wasn't my concern."

"Really? In Snowy Lake?" We were so far off the beaten track that that surprised me. Usually, people had friends or relatives in town to stay with if they were looking for a job. "Did the guy mention if he knew anyone here?"

"Yeah, his father worked a gold claim, then up and vanished one day when he was still a kid. He was still cut up about it. Now, if you're finished, I gotta get back to work. Tires don't fix themselves."

"His father?" My heart rate accelerated. The bones in the cave. *Can it be?* "What was his father's name? Did he say?"

"Terrance, I think. Why, what does it matter now?"

"He didn't happen to mention a treasure map?"

He froze. *You scoundrel. You're holding back evidence.* "Was it you out at Gold Mountain recently?"

"What are you talking about?" This time he was genuinely surprised before he grew suspicious. So, it wasn't him. I wasn't sure if I should mention the skeleton or if that should be kept secret.

"Did you share *everything* you know with the authorities?" I challenged.

"Sure, of course I did," he blustered, scratching his nose and looking away, a tell for someone most likely lying through their backside.

"Good. That's important so you're not seen to be aiding and abetting a criminal."

"What? I'm just a guy working an honest day's labor. You got no call to make me out some kind of master criminal. I just met the guy and that's all there was to it."

"If you say so, Buddy."

The dark glance that followed my skeptical words gave me an instant case of the willies.

"You're barking up the wrong tree, missy. Best take a look to your own family. I hear your aunt's taken off to parts unknown. Maybe the deaths were as simple as bad moonshine from her secret recipe?"

"That moonshine came from Sergei's operation, not Auntie T.J.'s, *after* he stole her recipe. Maybe he just didn't copy it correctly." I knew I shouldn't let him get to me, but my protective mode was near impossible to turn off. It was like some kind of laser strike field with a no-prisoners approach when it comes to my family.

"And maybe it was her actual product? Well, I guess we'll know soon enough when the toxicology report comes back what the real deal is." He gave a smirk, exposing crooked teeth that could use a cleaning. *Like last year.*

"We certainly will. And let me tell you something else, Buddy Harrison—I'll be keeping close tabs on you."

I just about jumped out of my skin as a voice suddenly spoke, hale and hearty, right behind me.

"Buddy, now what have you gone and done to get this lovely young lady so riled up about?" Floyd Millhouse asked, his tone banal. I'd missed his arrival.

Not good. I needed to stay more alert and keep my emotions out of it. I suddenly felt in need of a shower, remembering my last encounter with the man.

"Nothing. Just noting that her aunt's missing. She took it wrong is all." Buddy shrugged.

"You suggested my auntie had something to do with those two men's deaths."

Buddy remained mute, his lips twitching.

Floyd turned to me, not bothering to hide his interest in my figure. *Eww.* This guy should have been nicknamed the Hound Dog. *Hmm.* There was still time to nominate him.

"Have you heard anything new, Miss McCall, about the murders? I know you're *very* astute about human nature. Very gifted in fact, not to mention close friends with the constable." It seemed entirely appropriate now that these two men hung around together–they were both tremendous sleazeballs.

"There have been developments in the case, but that's all I can say. Constable Collins asked me to keep it quiet. He'll share when the time is right. And as you know, I'm a woman of my word." I added a calculated prissiness to my tone.

Floyd narrowed his eyes.

"Was there anything else you wanted?" Buddy asked.

Well, it looked like my job was done. I had royally pissed off both men. *Good. Emotional people make mistakes.* As much as I wanted to get a better reading on Buddy, I'd be keeping my distance from Floyd, knowing what he thought about ninety-nine-point-nine percent of the day.

"No, just tell Tug to drop off my Jeep at the Tea & Tarot. Thanks."

Buddy didn't say anything, so I took my leave. What Floyd was doing there, anyway? Of course, it was a tire shop, so probably just buying tires. My thoughts were confirmed when I went by the Lakeside Inn's van and noted a low tire on the front right passenger side.

I stood on Main Street, basking in the sunlight, and considered my next move. I had a chuckle at the new sign over the Snowy Lake Laundromat — *Pet Friendly, except bears. Won't make that mistake again.* Ted and Elsie were known for being animal lovers, but I guessed this time it had gone a touch too far.

Hmm. Did Ace know that Terrance Rail was the father of Jon Rail? My gut said those were his bones in the cave. It was sad to think that the boy, now a man, had come to town to check on the place that his father had vanished from so long ago and met the same fate.

The suspect list had tightened now. Floyd, Buddy and Eric were all contenders for the murders. Maybe they were in cahoots? Gold was a powerful motivator. And who had killed Terrance Rail so long agio? I shivered. *And to think the man's death had gone unpunished.* I shook my head. This needed to be solved yesterday.

My attention was caught by Tulip running full bore toward me down the sidewalk. I hurried to meet up with her.

"What is it, sis?"

"You need to come quick!" She was out of breath and stopped to take one, holding on to my arm for balance, her breath harsh in my ears. "April Harrison needs a reading from you in the worst way."

"Buddy's wife?" My ears perked up. That was an interesting development. "Why, what's up?"

"She wouldn't say. Just said it was important and she'd pay you double."

"You know April can be a bit of a drama queen, right?" I didn't know how Buddy actually put up with it, how his wife of eighteen months could go on about the smallest thing. The reality squeezed a bit of sympathy out of me as we scurried toward the café.

"Sure. But double payment isn't something to sniff at, right? You know, especially since things might be changing for a while."

I realized the last reference was in relation to our mother and the procedure we'd both be undergoing. No matter that we had universal healthcare in Canada, there were still unexpected expenses. Yes, she was right—best to step up our game now and sock some extra funds away.

"That reminds me. We need to send another cake out to Wild Horse Ranch later, keep George sweetened up." Sure, it was work we'd not be paid for, but some things, like keeping Ivana happy were worth more than money. I picked up my pace, beyond curious about what April wanted.

"There you are!" April's shrill voice greeted us soon as we burst through the front door of the café, the angel chimes squealing blue bloody murder over our heads as we raced by.

April was looking fine with her usual perfect hair and expensive-looking clothing that wouldn't be out of place if she were walking the runway at a New York fashion-week show. She hadn't started out her life like that but had been poor and living in a survivalist camp up north.

But since she'd come to live in Snowy Lake after turning eighteen and marrying Buddy, she'd been spending money like there was no tomorrow. I had no idea how they managed on his salary, and the fact she'd given up her service job. *Credit card debt?* Of course, it wasn't my concern, but I did like to understand the foibles of human nature.

"Sorry, I was away on an errand. Tulip said you wanted a reading? Did you lose something?"

"Yes! I'm about to tear my hair out."

I doubted it. "Come. We'll sit in the booth and deal with it straight away." I led the way to the midnight-blue fabric canopied booth with the extra-large gold star over the opening. Too bad April wasn't after a tarot reading or a dream interpretation. Star or Tulip could have done that for her.

We sat across from each other in the cozy interior. I laid my hands on the table.

"Okay, place your hands on mine, close your eyes and think about what it is you want to find."

She shimmied out of her white cashmere coat and let it fall back over the seat. She resettled herself by smoothing her thick auburn waves into perfect alignment, then adjusted her black pencil skirt and pink satin top with the lace collar and inserts, before she finally laid her hands atop mine. I couldn't help admiring how well the soft pink set off her thick auburn hair.

Out of the darkness came an image of a treasure map, like the aperture of a camera opening in a black and white, woman tied to the train tracks old movie footage. And not just any map, but the actual treasure map I had witnessed in Jon Rail's mind. I just about squealed out loud, giving the game away. I held on to my emotions with some difficulty, worried that my hands would begin sweating. That would make her pull away for certain.

"Did you see it? The map?" she asked with an excited tremor in her voice.

"*Yes*. Show me where you last saw it and anything else that can help me find it."

A view of the map that she obviously held in her hand, judging from the extra-large diamond on her ring finger, came into my mind. She was tucking the document inside a jewelry box hidden in the top drawer of a chiffonier. Then I got the next image of her lifting the lid again, and it was gone.

"Did you see it? Do you know where it is?"

"Yes, but I need a bit longer. Please, just relax and let the image linger in your mind. I'm catching something here..." *Where are you now, Mr. Treasure Map?*

The map reappeared, not in the same box, but in someone else's hands and being placed inside another dark place. Perhaps a safe or safe deposit box? Who was holding the map? The hands were definitely male, with large hairy knuckles, and the actions felt furtive. The person moved away, and I realized the safe was in a large room. I didn't recognize the space, but it might have been an office or living room. The wall behind the safe was painted the perfect Canadian beige, our unofficial national color. He covered the spot with a seascape painting, placing it over the opening to the safe to keep its location hidden. The painting appeared more paint-by-number than fine-artist rendered.

"A man took the map," I murmured.

"What man?" Her hands jerked as she sat up straighter.

"I can't see his face. He's turned away, hiding himself."

"Please, try harder. If I don't get that map back, it's going to be a *huge* problem for me. I'll pay you an extra-extra bonus."

"He put the map into a safe, but I don't recognize the room. But over the safe is a sixteen by twelve painting of a simple seascape. Then the connection broke down. I'm sorry."

"Is that all?" She sounded disgusted. "People pay you for *that*?"

"Generally. But if you're not satisfied, there's no charge." I swallowed as I said those hard words, knowing that our family needed the money more now than ever. What if I couldn't work for a while?

"Well, I'm *not* paying for that!"

"Hey, that's not fair," Tulip said, overhearing the loudly spoken words. "Charm gave you all she could, you know. Just because that's all there is to know doesn't mean you can just walk off without paying her." Her steely blue eyes were surprisingly annoyed for the easiest-going McCall triplet, according to popular vote.

April threw down a ten-dollar bill and left in a somewhat stylized huffy manner, meaning she looked like she'd had a lot of practice in the past.

"Well, I wasn't going to let her stiff you." Tulip looked more belligerent than I'd ever seen her about a customer.

"Thanks. But that was good information she brought me. Perhaps I should have been paying her," I mused.

"What?" She groaned. "After I just about ran her out of here?"

"Something else I know — her husband Buddy's not going to be too impressed with her coming to see me today when he finds out about her asking me to find a missing treasure map. And especially once he finds out that bones were discovered in the treasure map's location."

The angel chimes gave a happy burst of chatter as the door opened.

Chapter Twenty-One

Constable Ace Collins touched his Stetson in greeting, a smile lingering on his lips. Dang, every time I saw the guy, I swore he got more handsome. "How are my favorite ladies doing?"

Tulip winked at me. "Good, and you?"

"I'm well, thank you for asking. If I could have a word, Miss McCall?"

"I wonder which one of us he means?" Tulip teased before skipping away, leaving us alone.

"What's up, Sheriff?" I asked, teasing him back.

His eyes twinkled with amusement. "I'm not the sheriff, darlin'. Just a constable here on business."

"O-kay." *Business, eh.* But he didn't look upset, so it couldn't be something untoward, right? It was getting harder and harder to separate the parts of our lives, especially now that we were investigating crimes together.

He stilled, his expression sobering. "We now know the poison that killed the two men. The report from the ME just came in a half hour ago. The poison involved salts used in gold mining. Apparently, potassium cyanide reacts with gold to form soluble gold cyanide compounds that can be washed out of rocks and collected. The gold can then be easily extracted from its cyanide compounds. It was located in the jars of moonshine. So, I need to know if you've heard from your aunt?"

"Oh...boy." My stomach did a full three-sixty, making bile move upward to wash the back of my throat in acid. *Not good. Not good at all.* I scrambled about for a second. "I have information as well."

"Go ahead."

"I talked with Buddy at Tug's Tire Shop earlier. I think we might have a lead on the bones. Jon Rail's father, a guy called Terrance Rail, came to the town decades ago to goldmine. And Buddy knew about the treasure map. His wife, April, was in looking to see if I could find it. It was taken from her bedroom dresser."

"If Terrance Rail had a partner and he killed him, then it stands to reason that when the son comes to town and starts asking questions all these years later, that the murderer is in fear of being discovered. Fear is a powerful motivator in murder. We find Terrance Rail's original partner and we might have the name of the murderer for that crime and the new ones as well."

"That leaves Auntie T.J. off the hook, right?"

"Did she ever do any gold mining?"

"I'm not sure." I began to chew on my nonexistent thumbnail. *Cheez, you'd think they'd grow in a bit quicker.* "I'll have to ask Granny."

Ace nodded, then reached out and gently took the hand away from my mouth. "No need to worry. I don't think your aunt's a murderer. I just want to talk to her. Make sure we have all our facts straight."

"Thanks." I breathed a sigh of relief.

"But we do have a murderer on our hands. That worries me, especially since it appears that it's happened in the past. Shows a clear pattern. Of course, we have to wait for the DNA testing results for it to be conclusive if the two victims are related, but this is important evidence. Helpful to the case and is a very plausible scenario. But now, I'm worried."

"What about?"

"You. You've uncovered things that the murderer will not be happy about."

"*Phttt*, I'll be fine."

"Do you have any idea how very much you have come to mean to me, Miss McCall?"

"I'm starting to get it." I averted my eyes, shyness overcoming me. *Do you know how much I've fallen for you, handsome?* "But don't worry. McCalls can take care of themselves."

"But until we discover the killer, I want your word that you won't take chances."

"I don't take unnecessary chances."

"Right! And what do you call hiking to Gold Mountain on your own without a proper cell phone situation would be considered?"

"A wisely laid out strategy to gain intel on the current situation? I'm here, aren't I? Safe and sound."

He came a step closer, making all the moisture vanish from my mouth. The man was just so much. Big and strong and oh-so-over-the-top virile.

"I'm very happy that you're here. But I want your solemn promise, your hand on one of those grimoires you cherish so much, that you won't be running off again without informing me first. Is that too much to ask?"

"Ah, no. Not *that* much." I could compromise a tiny wee bit, considering how good he was about bringing me the details so quickly on the cause of death, and pretty much saying my auntie was innocent, even though she'd gone AWOL. It was one of the biggest trade-offs that I'd ever agreed with Ace about, and it gave me pause. Were we really taking our relationship to another level? Was I ready for that? *Oh yeah.*

"Thank you." He gave that slow sexy smile of his and patted his chest. "My heart thanks you as well, since I'd prefer not to be taken out by a bad ticker. I'll catch you later."

"Only if you have on good track shoes!"

We shared another smile and out he strolled to the sound of the angel chorus singing a rousing addition of *O Canada.*

The rest of the day passed in s-l-o-w motion, my glances at the rooster clock increasing by the quarter hour. Somehow, today, once Ace had departed, the tedium had hit. Was that another sign he was the right one for me? The one who guaranteed that I would keep all my goddess-given gifts after we, *aw*, finally, got to home base?

When closing time came, I locked up, then headed into the back to bake. Since my sisters had stepped up yesterday, today was my turn to make sure we had enough food prepared on hand for the morning. Both my sisters had made themselves scarce this afternoon, though I had a pretty good idea where they were. Maybe I'd drop by later, see if my healing was still helping? *What's wrong with right now?*

Mind made up, I removed my apron and set it aside, then put one foot in front of the other and walked out of the door. Two minutes later, outside Auntie T.J.'s house, I stood on the sidewalk, trying to work up the courage to go inside. As I dithered, an eagle flew overhead drawing my attention. *Okay. Message received.*

"Hey, Star."

My sister looked up from her perch on the sofa where she was watching TV as I entered the front door.

"What are you doing here?" Her blue eyes narrowed. She lowered the volume on the television set and got up.

"Thought maybe it was time for a visit."

"She's sleeping, last I checked."

"Okay, I'll come back later." I turned to go, relieved to just go home and bake, when a voice called out from the other room.

"Charm, is that you?"

"Want me to go in with you?" Star asked, surprising me.

"No, thanks. I should do this alone."

She nodded. "I'll be here if you need me." She sat and turned up the volume on the TV show.

"Thanks."

The few tense baby steps down the hallway took the most courage of all. What was I going to say to her? How could there possibly be any excuse for our upbringing that would bring some resolution? What if there wasn't any? Would seeing her just all be in vain? Dig up stuff that was best left buried?

I almost didn't make it that last step into the open doorway. *Goddess, grant me the serenity to head into this whirlwind.*

"Charm, it that you? Come in where I can see you."

My heart hammering in my chest, I walked the last mile.

The woman in the bed was improved. At least her eyes had more life in them, searching mine for answers.

I dutifully moved through the doorway and sat on a chair near the bed.

"Hi, Mom."

"It's good to see you, sweetheart."

I had nothing to say to that. I felt nothing good at the moment. Just conflicted and as uncomfortable as I could be. I chewed on a fingernail, searching around for something to say.

"You still do that."

"What?"

"Bite your fingernails."

I dropped my hand. "So, you're feeling better?"

"I am, thanks to you. I hear I have something else to thank you for."

"What's that?"

"For donating a kidney."

"Yeah, well, I can't have Star doing that." Anger fueled my words. "She's got a bright future to look forward to and I don't want her touched by all this." I gestured tersely with my hand at her, indicating her sickness and her need for us now.

She chewed on her bottom lip, a frown creasing her forehead. "I didn't want this. I almost didn't come home."

"Then why did you?" The words came out harsher than I'd intended. *Or maybe not.*

She broke eye contact with me then and began picking at the comforter that covered her. "I wanted to see my girls. You know, before I passed on."

"We're not your girls. Granny's raised us longer than we were ever with you." My head began to throb, my body trembling with too much emotion.

"I am grateful for that. At least you had a decent life with her."

"Why, *why* did you want drugs more than us?" The big question come out of a sudden and lay right there in the room between us like a giant black spider.

"Oh, Charm, it's something I've asked myself a million times. My life has been so messed up. I've made so many mistakes. I was too young when I had you three. I wasn't ready to be a mother."

"You don't get to say that as your excuse. Lots of women have babies young and manage. You could have at least *tried*. You didn't ever look like you cared at all, always leaving us and going out. Leaving us locked up in the dark." Stark images from the past swirled in my brain, a kaleidoscope of seething pain.

"I was afraid you would wander outside and get hurt. I didn't have anyone to call on to stay with you. No friends, no family. I was all alone."

"You don't think we weren't hurt being shut up like that? Star still has nightmares." *Me too.*

"I know saying I'm sorry will never be enough." Her voice broke and I looked at her. Tears were running down her sunken cheeks. "No amount of being sorry can fix this. But all I want is a chance to try to make it better from now on. Try to make a few new memories. I'm clean now. No drugs for over six months."

At least that's something.

"And I don't want you giving me a kidney. Not if you feel this way." She shook her head. "It might be best if I let nature take its course. I haven't earned the right to ask, I see that now. I was a terrible mother. I caused you all such horrible pain. There is no forgiveness for that. No way to fix it or move on."

Her calmly spoken words took my breath away. She was giving herself a death sentence and her fortitude shocked me. Maybe she really had changed.

Take back your power. Forgiveness is the way. Ace's words came back to me then.

"I don't think I can ever forget what happened. But maybe, we can start again. I—I don't want you to die."

I wouldn't let a stranger die without my help, I certainly couldn't do that to family. "So, I will willingly give you a kidney. And maybe we can start to make some new memories? Or at least try to."

"Oh, sweetheart. You have no idea what your words mean to me." Her shoulders shook with emotion. I had to bite down hard on my cheek not to break into tears myself.

"Charm, is everything okay?" Star stood in the doorway.

I gave my sister a reassuring smile, my headache easing. "Yeah, everyone's fine."

I got to my feet. "I gotta go home and bake. We're low on some desserts at the café."

I chanced a glance at our mother. She nodded and swiped at her eyes before blowing her nose with a tissue. "Go on. I'll be fine. Thanks for coming, sweetheart. It meant the world to me."

Star walked me to the front door. "Are you really going home to bake? Now?"

"Definitely. I'll see you tomorrow."

I stepped out into the fresh fall air and took a deep breath. A load lifted from my shoulders as I strode back along the sidewalk. Yes, time to move ahead. We had made a little progress today. Who knew where it would lead? How much it would affect the future? But, in this moment, things looked brighter. I couldn't ask for more than that.

* * * *

Baking. The familiar motions of assembling, measuring, stirring and pouring batter. That was the only way to keep my mind off what couldn't be changed. By midnight, I had enough food stashed to feed the military if they needed to set up camp in our town. It could happen, thinking of the awful deluge of 2013 when the water came within inches of flooding out the entire area. The valiant efforts of so many willing hands had stacked sandbags, preventing disaster. After the danger had passed, our whole town had stepped up and thrown a turkey dinner with all the trimmings in their honor.

I tucked the last tray of cookies into a container, turned off the lights and headed up to my apartment. Too tired to do more than brush my teeth, I fell onto my bed and pulled the comforter over me, dead to the world in a split second.

Something woke me and I forced my gritty eyes to open. Groggy from an extreme lack of sleep, I checked the bedside clock. Three a.m. I waited, listening. *Darn it.* Someone was in the kitchen, moving about and knocking into things. Ivana? Sometimes she rummaged for food after being out half the night doing whatever it was that she did. I didn't ask, preferring to keep my head on my shoulders. But I stumbled from my bed anyway, pulled on my Hello Kitty robe and staggered into the hallway, headed for the kitchen.

Halfway down the staircase, the noises escalated, and I hurried my step. *What the fudge!* The kitchen was in complete disarray. Someone, dressed in a black ski mask of all things, was throwing things around. Cupboard doors were standing open, items strewn on counters and even the floor. The complete disregard for it being a place of hygienic business made my blood about boil.

"What do you think you're doing?" I picked up a heavy cast-iron frypan and advanced on the culprit, raising it high above my head. The invader, definitely a man judging by his size and circumference and about double my size, stopped dead in their tracks. They'd left off the overhead lights, but had a flashlight clutched in one gloved hand. The nightlights in a couple of the electrical outlets also helped us to see each other. I had them placed there as I didn't want Ivana falling on one of her midnight raids and suing us for breaking her tidy behind.

"Where is it?" the person growled, standing firm.

"What?" I moved a step closer, ready to swing the solid device at their head with the slightest provocation.

"The treasure map. The one you stole."

"I didn't steal any map. What on earth gave you that idea?" Was it Buddy standing there? Or maybe Eric or Floyd? They were all of similar stature. It was really hard to be sure with all the black, bulky clothing and the dim lighting. He'd turned off his flashlight and the night lights weren't enough. The full-head ski mask hid so darn much. My fingers fairly itched to tear the article from his head, but they were occupied holding the frypan over his head.

"You know where it is." His tone grew more menacing. "Tell me or so help me I'll —"

"Or you'll what?" I moved a step closer yet, standing with my feet the proper distance apart, the weight evenly distributed over my legs, like we trained for in our coven in our ongoing self-defense courses that Ace had assisted us with on occasion.

He hesitated, then turned and made his escape. I went to follow him, racing as far as the alleyway and looking down it as he fled on foot. I thought better of it ten seconds later, shivering from the cold, and stomped back inside the kitchen, turning on the overhead lights.

Oh, blast it! The kitchen was in a dreadful state. The guy should have been made to stay and clean up the mess he'd made. That would be proper justice. I tried closing the door, but it wouldn't lock. He'd damaged it by forcing his way inside. Well, at least I couldn't be blamed for leaving the door unlocked. I imagined what Ace would have to say about *that*.

No help for it though. I had to call this in. I picked up the phone and dialed Ace's home number instead of the detachment. It was better not to have an official visit with sirens blazing in the middle of the night and waking everyone.

"Hello." His sleepy tone was beyond endearing, but I would have enjoyed it more on any other type of occasion than a failed robbery.

"Ace, it's Charm."

"What's wrong?" His voice was instantly alert.

"There's been a break-in at the café." I trembled, the catch in my voice obvious. Why was it always worse when it was said out loud? Someone had broken in. *Invaded my space.* I was angry and a tiny bit afraid.

"I'll be right there." The line went dead. I carefully put the receiver back into its cradle and surveyed the dismal mess.

"Darn it." A large sack of flour had broken open and the white stuff was strewn all over, covering pots and pans with flour grit. I sighed and went to the cleaning cupboard to pull out the vacuum. It would take up the worst of it before I had the huge job of washing everything. At three in the morning.

"Cheez, if you wanted a copy of the darn map so bad, you could have just asked. I would have drawn one for you." I perched on a stool, drumming my fingers on the countertop, as antsy as all get out. I'd need to get the lock fixed as well in the morning. There was no point in calling the insurance agent. Rising premiums would be the end result. *Better to just take care of it myself.*

Ace burst through the disabled door, his clothing more in disarray than I'd ever seen it — shirt untucked, boots unlaced, no jacket on a chilly fall night.

He hurried over through the maze of stuff thrown about and gathered me into his arms. I went willingly. "Are you all right?" He peered into my face, pushing back the thick strands of hair that had fallen free of my nighttime braid.

I took a deep breath, breathing in his stabilizing scent of gorgeous man. "Better, thanks." I hiccupped. "I think I could use a glass of water."

He hugged me for a long moment, then moved away to fill a tumbler with tap water, handing it to me. "Thanks." I downed it and took a deep breath. "I would have drawn the guy a map if he'd only asked."

"He spoke?"

"Yeah, didn't like the fact I might be hiding the treasure map."

"Do you think it was Buddy Harrison?"

"Maybe." I shrugged and put down the empty glass. "I couldn't be sure. He was dressed all in black and wearing a ski mask."

Ace scowled. "When I get my hands on who did this, so help me…"

"Who else wanted it? Maybe Eric or Floyd? They're all of a similar height and body shape."

"They're all on my list. Okay, I'll take care of the lock first."

"You don't need to do that now. I can just use a knife stabbed between the doorframe and that will work until morning."

"I insist." His extra-strong tone suggested arguing was futile. "Do you have any tools?"

I went and retrieved the box of odds and ends we kept under the sink for manual jobs and he set to work. As I vacuumed, my mind went over the strange encounter. The map wasn't hard to remember once a person had figured out about where the X was located, but why would they want it so badly? What was the significance of the map? There had to be something more to wanting the actual physical map. I needed to locate it, certain that somehow it would lead to the killer.

An hour of intense concentration on both our parts and the place was presentable, though I was most unhappy about throwing away the damaged baking supplies. I shook my head at the garbage bag filled with now-useless items. *Such a waste.* I loathed waste with every fiber of my being. It came from being hungry as a kid, I would imagine. I didn't need a therapist to figure that out.

"There we go. All fixed." Ace surveyed his work, trying the deadbolt again to make certain it was set into the door frame properly. "I'll just touch up the paint tomorrow. Try it now and see if it closes easily enough for you. I can adjust it if not."

"Sure." I dutifully opened and reclosed the door. "Perfect, you'd never know it happened. Thanks."

"No problem." He looked around. "Looks like you're back in business."

"You know, that map is important to the case. Maybe there's something written on the back of it? I would *love* to get my hands on it for two seconds. If someone wants it badly enough to break in, then it must have a clue that leads to the murderer. Stands to reason, right?"

"Miss McCall, I want your solemn promise to stay out of it and not ask any more questions about the darn map. Look what happened here! Accosted in the middle of the night over it. No, I won't hear of it." Ace looked loaded for bear, his jaw set like granite. Oh boy, when he got like that, it was best to just let him rant. That much I had learned in the months since he'd come to our town.

"Okay, well, when it turns up, I'm sure it will provide a clue." I kept my voice noncommittal.

He ran his hands through his disheveled hair. He'd be adorable, if he hadn't been so thoroughly annoyed looking. "Your safety *is* my number one concern."

"Is it now?" I smiled to soften the blow. "I thought doing your job was your number one concern?"

"Don't test me, darlin'."

Our glances met and locked. A wild spark leaped between us and the lightbulb blew out over the sink in a bright flash of stars, pitching that side of the room into darkness.

"Shoot, not again. You're costing me a ton of replacement bulbs, Officer."

"I'll pay my way." He came a few steps closer and gathered me in his arms. I snuggled against him, breathing in his essence. We stood pressed together for a few seconds and I regained my equilibrium. Ace had the affect on me. I wasn't complaining, just leery about what the future held for us.

"I am wanting this case concluded so I can take you away."

"It's going to be nice." I didn't want to break away from the hug, our heartbeats echoing in perfect tandem through our clothing.

"Now, you need to get to bed. Have a few hours of sleep or you'll be tired all day tomorrow. And that can lead to bad decisions."

"You too." I broke away reluctantly. How long until I gave in to my desires? I took a deep breath. I didn't know, but it was getting harder and harder to resist the man.

I saw him out and locked the door, knowing he was lingering on the other side, waiting to hear the deadbolt make its decisive sound of striking home. Smiling to myself, I climbed the stairs to my apartment. A few hours of sleep sounded like heaven. And knowing Ace had my back was priceless.

Chapter Twenty-Two

"What's the deal for tomorrow, sis? Are we ready?" Tulip asked.

I looked up from adding a binding spell to a special trinket for Ace's Promise Bag, unable to keep a broad smile from quirking my lips. "*Oh yeah*, we're ready." After spending an hour or three calming down my family, then each and every Northern Lights coven member after they heard about *the incident*, as we now referred to it, I had gotten around to finishing up all the pressing items for the event of the week, the Sadie Hawkins dance.

"Good. It's been such a crazy week that I don't think I could stand another thing going off-kilter." Tulip gave a long, suffering sigh. Then something must have grabbed her attention on her computer screen, because she gave a loud squeal. "Oh my gosh! Look at this. An order for fifty dozen of our special brownies."

I groaned. Just when I thought I was caught up. "Fifty dozen? I doubt we have more than five dozen single-wrapped in the freezer. That's a lot of edibles. Who's placing the order?"

"Huh, someone in town. Eric Taylor. Maybe he's branching out from only having moonshine available?"

"Eric. One of our prime suspects. Better get a deposit on the order." What if his hiney was dragged off to the jail? We'd be stuck with far more product than we could sell in a month of Sundays.

"He did better than that. He's already paid the full amount."

"Really? *Please, please* don't tell me he wants them all right this minute." I stopped what I was doing and stared at my sister, praying that we had some lead time on making a ton of brownies. Though it was nice that we could charge more for them, they took longer to make to get the amount of concentrated marijuana cannabutter just right to abide by Federal regulations, something that only I had become an expert at. *So, three guesses as to who most of the job will fall to?*

"Ah, yeah, he wants them to be delivered tomorrow afternoon." Tulip gave me a patented I'm-so-sorry look from over her computer monitor.

"Of course, he does," I muttered.

"Oh, my goodness!" Her eyes looked about to bug out of her beautiful face.

"What is it now?"

"Another huge order!"

"No! Just say no!" The irony of Nancy Reagan's catch phrase for the war on drugs currently ongoing south of the border and coming out of my mouth didn't escape me.

"I can't! They've already paid up too. Shirley Millhouse. And she wants *sixty* dozen."

The two of us stared at each other, too flabbergasted to say a word.

"Shut it down. Now! Put an out-of-order sign up. Say we've suspended operations for a few days."

"Okay, I'll do what I can." Tulip's fingers fairly flew over the keyboard. "Yikes! Another one slipped through."

I groaned, wanting to smash her computer to bits, then raced to peer over her shoulder. "Who now?"

"Buddy Davidson."

"How many?"

"Ah, only thirty-five dozen."

"*Only* thirty-five – " Panic rose in my voice. "Do you know how many that is in total? One hundred and forty-five dozen special brownies. Each one hand wrapped and labeled. Do you know how long that will take us? It cannot be physically done in time. I'm going to have to go over and see them in person, and tell them it's freakin' impossible."

I shook my head so hard that I must have given myself a concussion. Where was all this coming from? The two main suspects in the murder investigation and the wife of the third one, and all three had placed such ridiculously high orders? Was it to keep me too busy to look into their involvement in the investigation? Were they all in cahoots? *Way to give it away guys, if that's the deal.* But it also was going to be a very busy weekend with all the outsiders coming into town for the Homecoming dinner tonight and the dance tomorrow. And any businessperson worth their salt would want to make the most of the opportunity. Were they maybe looking to resell our product on the side?

"Okay, you get started and I'll go and see if I can stall them." I raced to nab my jacket hanging in the kitchen, just about plowing Tulip down as I ran by her, struggling to shove my arms into the proper sleeve. "Oops, sorry. I'll be back in ten."

I raced down the street, my body fueled by the immense power of a surge of extreme adrenaline. *Who first?* Boyd's wife, Shirley. A woman would better understand our time crunch dilemma.

Two minutes later, I rounded the corner of Telegraph Road and headed north down toward Third Street. Boyd and Shirley's large two-storey house stood on the corner. I glanced at Auntie T.J.'s house on the way by. Where was that woman? *Great time to abandon us.*

I rang the doorbell, jumping impatiently from foot to foot.

"Charm." Shirley greeted me soon as she opened the door. Her pale face was framed by a thick brown bob of smooth hair. "What a lovely surprise." Shirley was a sweet woman. She and Boyd had one daughter, hers from a previous marriage. There had been rumors of trouble in the marriage for years, but I wasn't one for gossip, so I didn't know any specific details. Anyone curious would have to ask Auntie T.J. for any and all particulars.

"Hey, Shirley. Can I come in?" I realized I had not been inside her home before. We'd always visited at the café or met in a store and exchanged pleasantries.

"Of course." She turned and led the way into the living room.

"That was some order you placed this morning." I stopped dead in my tracks in the doorway. There, on the opposite wall, was the seascape painting I had discovered in my reading for June yesterday.

"What order?"

"Ah, the order for the sixty dozen special brownies. That was you, right?" Was this some kind of joke being played on the McCall triplets by some prankster in town? We were not amused!

"Oh, I imagine that was Boyd. He was talking about it this morning. He likely used my account for the financial transaction. Business thing. I'll call him, if you like?"

"Please, if you don't mind? It's just that it's a lot of product and we need a bit more time to produce it all. I wanted to discuss an extension with you." My mind was on the painting. Wouldn't hurt to admire it, right?

I walked over to the far wall. "What a lovely seascape."

"Thanks. My sister painted it. If you want, she takes custom orders? If you'll excuse me, I'll just go and call Boyd. Be back in a jiff."

I moved closer and laid my hand on the painting then closed my eyes and willed the treasurer map to appear. *Yes. You're in hidden in there, you rascal.*

"What are you doing here?" The harsh question made me startle and whirl right around. Boyd had entered the living room and his dark ferret eyes were boring into mine. My mouth went dry.

"I came to see your wife."

"Where's Shirley?"

"Trying to call you, actually. I got a large order this morning that will be difficult to fill as it's not the only one we received at the last minute, and I came by to ask for an extension of time."

Shirley came back into the room, thank goodness. "Boyd, Charm was just saying how much she admired the painting that Doris did. Why are you being so abrupt with her?" Shirley looked from him to me, a look of apology in her tone and expression. She was way too nice to be married to this man.

He cracked a smile that didn't reach his eyes. "Excuse me, Miss McCall. Just on edge today. Work's been crazy busy and now you're saying you can't get the order done in time. I was counting on it to sell to all the people arriving today and tomorrow." He gave a sigh of frustration.

"Well, we'll do the best we can for you. It's just that two other orders almost as large came in and there's just no way we can get so much done so quickly."

"Fine. Do what you can." He smiled a bit nicer and gave his wife a quick peck on the cheek. "I just came by to check on you. What with all these murders, I worry, sugar."

Shirley blushed. "That's fine, Boyd. I'm safe as can be."

"Okay, I'm out of here. Whatever you can manage, Charm, I would appreciate it." Boyd stomped out and I heard the front door close behind him.

"Oh, that man. Such a romantic."

Romantic. Not the word I'd use. "Yes. He's something all right."

"So, you like Doris's work. She'll be thrilled. She just took up painting last summer and really needs to have her work displayed. She'll probably do it for cheap if you put it up at the Tea & Tarot. I have some of her paintings stored in the back, and you can even have one of those right now, if you like?"

I should have known better. *Never offer false compliments. It'll always bite you.*

"Great. Yes. Let's talk." Twenty minutes later, the proud owner of a mud-brown cabin in the woods painting tucked under my arm, I hurried back down the street. I'd chosen it for the sole reason of the dubious impression of Gold Mountain off in the distance.

"Charm! What took you so long?" Tulip greeted me as I walked in the back door. She had ingredients spread out every available surface, her expression beyond desperate.

"I bought us some time on Boyd and Shirley's order." I showed her the painting.

"That's not going up here, is it?"

"Afraid so."

"I should call the other two men. Let them know our dilemma." I stood and debated with myself. *Jump in or buy time?*

"I'll take care of that. You're better at the brownies than I am." Tulip raced for the telephone. "And I'll call in the troops. See who's available?"

I headed for the sink and washed my hands. It was going to be a long, long day and probably just as long a night. So much for a nice, peaceful Homecoming meal with friends and family.

My sister's voice droned on and on as she made the calls. I tuned her out and set to work.

"Okay, I made a good deal with the other two who ordered from us. Half now, and half for next weekend. Halloween's a good time for treats like these too. You know, for the adult parties."

"Good job." I made the calculations in my brain. "Okay, that means seventy-two and a half dozen needed. Oh, and we have five dozen on hand. That means we need to prepare eight hundred and ten individually wrapped brownies."

"And Star will be here soon with James and a couple of the coven members who can get away."

"Great. That helps." If the idea was to keep me from sleuthing and hard at work in the kitchen, they'd won this round. *But be warned, I'm not letting go of this investigation anytime soon.* I needed to get my hands on the map. Oh, I knew just how to upset that apple cart...

I picked up the phone and dialed June's number. "I just got a lead on that map you were after."

"Really? Where is it?" Her breathless voice filled my head.

"Boyd's got it in his safe."

Dead silence. "Well, thanks for telling me. Maybe it was worth the money after all. I'll see you later."

"Yes, let me know what you find out." I grinned ear to ear, imagining the showdown.

The buoyed-up feeling kept me sailing right through the creation of dozens of delicious brownies. Though I missed the Homecoming dinner, just sending Star and James along to deliver the cakes and assorted desserts, I hardly noticed my aching feet or back.

A brisk knock on the back door and in strolled Ace. He took one look at the flurry of activity before weaving his way over to me. "I missed you at dinner." He leaned down and gave me a quick kiss on the cheek. His lips were warm and inviting, and a zing of energy shot right through me.

"Me too. But we had some late orders that needed filling." I poured the final batter of the evening into a large tray and set it in the oven. "There, last batch for tonight. Thanks, everyone, for the tremendous help. I got this now. Go home and sleep."

My tired crew washed up and vanished in a matter of seconds. I glanced at the rooster clock. *Midnight.*

"You got some flour on your nose." Ace reached and dusted it away before winking at me. "Not that you don't look cute as a button no matter what."

I grinned at him. "So, anything new?"

"Still investigating." He sighed. "Those suspects have been well coached in what to say, in my opinion. Like a closed club."

"I know where the original map is." Before he could say anything, I filled him in.

"Interesting." I could see the cogs turning and rotating every which way in his brain. I would desperately love to see deeper inside that marvelous brain of his, but I kept myself from invading his space. It would be wrong on so many levels.

"I imagine all Hades broke loose after that," I quipped.

"You'd never know it. The town's quiet, just like I prefer it to be."

"Wait until tomorrow night. Things are about to heat *way* up. The Sadie Hawkins dance will be a ton of fun. I guarantee it."

"No hints about what awaits me?"

"You'll just have to wait and see, handsome."

His eyes lit up with my new moniker for him. "Then I will just have to be patient, beautiful." He gathered me in his arms and I hugged him back just as tightly, my one minute of pure bliss for the day.

"Something else too. I talked with my mom last night."

"How did that go?" He drew back a bit to look me in the eyes.

"Better than I expected, actually. Something you said helped. About trying to forgive? I think I made my first tiny baby step in that direction. She surprised me, saying she wasn't going to take one of my kidneys if I wasn't ready. It made me realize I did want time to try to make a few new memories — better ones."

"That's really good to hear. I'm so proud of you, Charm."

"Thanks."

I heard the sonic drill of high heels on the floor and inwardly groaned. Ivana was home.

"Take pity with man. Make love soon — in bed. Rock his world," she said, her expression as mischievous as a demented pixie's. She nodded upward at the ceiling, pointing one red-tipped fingernail above her head in case we didn't completely understand.

We broke apart.

"I should be going." Ace avoided my eyes and left in a flash.

Flustered, I turned toward her, hands on hips. "Ivana, that's not helping."

"Ah, but Charm not let Ivana help best friend. Big man — big needs." She widened her cat-shaped eyes at me, innocent as all get-out, and headed upstairs. I narrowed my eyes. Something told me that woman knew better English than she let on. She just loved to yank chains. I was becoming more and more certain of it. Not that it would change the picture one wit. No one confronted Ivana past a certain point.

Chapter Twenty-Three

I surveyed myself in the bathroom mirror. After another crazy day had been spent baking, icing and wrapping dozens of brownies, and we'd come to close to fulfilling the orders. A sense of pride washed through me at how hard we'd all worked to get the job done. Everyone with a free hour or two had stepped up, though Auntie T.J. had remained absent.

The Sadie Hawkins affair beckoned in less than a half hour. I'd had to cancel my hair and makeup appointment, making do with my own limited skills. I hurriedly applied a layer of pink lip gloss that I was certain Susie would scoff at, with my intense coloring. She'd always insisted red was the perfect lip color for me, but I'd never gotten around to buying a tube. Something else to add to my growing list of things to do before my upcoming vacation with Ace. My expression softened in the glass. Now, that was something to savor.

I checked my party dress one last time in the mirror, admiring the flow of the full skirt, the red silky fabric swishing around my knees as I twirled on my kitten heels, then skipped down the stairs to the café.

"Hey, sis, do you want me to load all the Promise Bags in your Jeep?" Tulip asked. She was dressed in a pink lace frock that suited her still tan-in-October skin and shiny blonde hair. On her a pink lip gloss similar to mine looked beyond amazing. I sighed, thinking how often I wished I was taller, slimmer and blonde like Star and Tulip. But it had not been meant to be.

I reminded myself I needed to concentrate on getting my hot little hands on the treasure map. With everyone expected at the dance tonight, the perfect opportunity was bound to present itself. I jumped into helping my sister load the precious boxes of surprises into Thor, my good humor fully restored.

"I'll meet you there," Tulip said, scurrying back inside the café, her curls flying.

I drove down the alley and headed for the Snowy Lake Centennial Hall where the dance was being held. The space has a wonderful dance floor, plenty of tables and chairs and room for most of the townspeople.

Pulling into the parking lot, I spied Ace's RCMP cruiser already in attendance. He was probably checking on the liquor permit and number of tickets sold. I grabbed the first box of Promise Bags, closed Thor's door with my foot and headed inside the hall.

The awesome Mountie greeted me just inside the doorway as he was leaving, still in uniform and looking good.

"Hey there, handsome."

"Pretty dress for a pretty lady."

"Thanks." I gave an impromptu curtsy, careful not to spill anything from the box. "We aim to please."

"I'll be back soon. I need to shower and dress in civilian clothes. I think it best when receiving one of those bags, that I'm not in uniform?"

"Wouldn't make one wit of difference. Place your mind at ease. I have no intention of embarrassing you."

"Great, then I have your word on that." He did indeed look relieved. What on earth had he thought I was going to give him as my suggestion of what I wanted from him? An engagement ring? Unbidden, the idea just popped into my mind, and I pushed the crazy thought right out again.

"You do, Ace. I would never intentionally embarrass you."

"Or I you, Miss McCall."

I watched him stroll away, his uniform demonstrating just how well-built he was. I sighed. *What an awesome hiney.*

"There you are!" My best friend Emma came rushing up, her normally unruly red hair fashioned into a sleek updo. She'd been away for a few days on a buying trip to Winnipeg for her new store, Valentine's Candy Shoppe, scheduled to open soon. The time away had agreed with her. She looked happy and carefree. Having just lost her auntie a few months back, she'd been at a loss for what to do with her life and had discovered her muse in the candy business. I understood. *Nothing like offering treats to others to bring a smile to your heart.*

I set my box down on the special white tableclothed table prepared in advance for the Promise Bags and grabbed her in a big bear hug. "I missed you so much! You look fabulous. Who did your hair?"

"Suzie, right here in town. Still the best hairdresser for me. You look wonderful as well. Gosh, I heard about the murders." She lowered her voice, glancing

January Bain

furtively around at the few people who were milling around the kitchen preparing for the evening.

"Yeah, been a bit nuts lately. But we're getting closer to solving it."

"*We*, eh. Tell me all about it." Her green eyes lit up with an inner fire.

I quickly filled her in on the facts. "But I mostly need to get my hands on that map."

"Can I help?"

"Can you keep an eye out for me?"

She nodded. "No problem." She held out her hand and we locked pinkies like we'd been doing since grade three when we'd bonded over show-and-tell, and I'd defended her choice of Eddie the rat. Sure, he wasn't a fancy white one from the pet store, but one from her backyard. Not his fault he was born a common local rat. "Pinky swear."

She linked arms with me. "Now let's get Thor unloaded. I can't wait for the games to begin."

"Me too." We skipped outside and grabbed a box each.

"What's in the box?" Brodie Jones, a slingshot hanging from his back pocket, sidled up to me, his blond brush cut showing off his brash face.

"Never you mind, Brodie," Emma said, giving him a small frown of warning. "Nothing in here for children. It's an adults-only box."

His light blue eyes opened wider. "Are those the things that make men go crazy? Do all kinds of icky, lovey-dovey things?"

"No one can make you do anything you don't want to do. It's just suggestions and ideas, Brodie," I said with a smile.

"My daddy says different. That it's all girly and witchy."

"No offense to your daddy, but there's nothing untoward going on," Emma said, striding past the young boy known to be one of the biggest mischief makers in Snowy Lake.

"Don't worry, Brodie. Nobody's going to do anything they don't want to do."

He trailed me to the entranceway, then held the door open for me.

"Why, thank you most kindly, young sir."

He grinned and hurried right in behind me, then raced past at full tilt, heading for the kitchen. I hoped his mother or father or some family member was in evidence. Who knew what the young hooligan-in-training would get up to if no one kept an eye on him? And that was what just his mother called him.

I adjusted the long white tablecloth covering the long banquet table that I would be displaying the bags on. Each had a hand-printed label pinned to the top of the midnight blue velvet that announced the woman's name and the name of the man it was intended for.

One hundred and seventeen bags in total. *Sweet. Best collection to date.* I stepped back and admired my handiwork from another angle. The artifacts and accompanying spells had taken many hours of preparation, but I didn't regret one second of it. This was one of the highlights of Snowy Lake's yearly wheel.

I spun around at the sound of high heels drilling holes in the hardwood floor.

"Best buddy. Have need. Come." Ivana grabbed at my arm, caught the limb in a vise-hold and began tugging me along the slippery floor like I was a sack of spuds for crafting specialty vodka.

"Hold on! Where are you dragging me off to?" I was pleased to see she was fully dressed in a vivid emerald-green stretchy number that contained enough of her ample assets to keep tonight's venue legal at least. After her comment on Putin and being bare-breasted on a horse, I had been a touch nervous. I had even brought along a few choice bits of fancy clothes in a bag left on Thor's backseat, just in case.

"Bathroom. Now. Charm needs makeover. Pink lip gloss with red dress? *Tsk-tsk.*"

"It's okay. I'm fine." Really, it wasn't the crime of the century, right, a chaste pink lip gloss?

She hauled me inside the hall's massive women's bathroom and over to the sink.

"Hold still." She pulled a makeup bag from her purse and opened it, selecting a slender tube of lipstick. She applied it to my lips, then commanded, "Make kissy face."

"What?"

"Smack lips together. Like this." She pressed her lips together.

I did what she demanded, then looked in the oval mirror over the sink. I actually looked good. Red was my color.

"Thanks. I like it."

She beamed like I had bestowed the finest compliment in the world. She struck her breast a solid blow over her heart, one of her famous moves. "Best friends."

"What's the color name? I'd like to buy it. Did you buy it here in town?"

"*Pssst. Pssst.*" Something or someone was going flat or trying desperately to get our attention from inside a stall.

"For you. Present." She pressed the lipstick tube into my hand.

"That's nice of you. I owe you one."

Her eyes lit up like dancing stars. "Excellent. I shall hold you to that."

Her English had improved dramatically and I narrowed my eyes at her.

"*Pssssssssssssssssst.*"

The sounds of someone about to have a coronary if I didn't respond distracted me from further discussion. I walked over and pushed open the stall door. Auntie T.J., her head swathed in a scarf like an old-style movie star, and an extra-large pair of sunglasses covering her eyes, stood waiting for me. Her clothing was hidden by a nondescript trench coat in ubiquitous beige. Rubber ducky boots completed the spiffy wardrobe.

"What are you doing here? Where have you been?"

"Have you solved the crime yet?" She sounded out of breath. I'm not certain it was because of her clandestine use of the facilities or her excitement at pretending to be a world-class spy.

"No. But we're getting closer."

A big theatrical sigh punctuated her words. "I thought you'd have figured it out by now, for heaven's sake! Between my brainiac niece and the clever Mountie. Cheez, Louise." She shook her head in disgust, her lips pursing into a pout. "Now I got to keep hiding out. Solve it already, will you!" She exited the stall, and before I could stop her, fled the bathroom. *Slippery as an eel, that one.*

"Auntie pain."

"You can say that again." I rolled my eyes, deciding to ignore her reversal in speaking the Queen's English. I also had too much to do to chase my auntie's hiney all over town. At least I knew she was okay.

"I go find date."

I glanced at the clock. "Yes, everyone should be arriving about now." As soon as the right people were in attendance, off I would go on my own planned rendezvous. Tonight, I just might find out the name of the murderer and uphold my reputation of being the town's designated brainiac, goddess willing.

We exited the bathroom and went our separate ways. Ivana headed to the bar while I went in search of Emma. I was pleased to see the room had filled with happy, excitedly chatting people in the last few minutes. Most had drinks in hand and were busy milling about, deciding which table to have a seat at. The right choice was deemed essential and required plenty of discussion. There was a protocol involved. *Choose the correct table and you get served first.* Roulette, really, as the organizers seemed to choose a different pattern every time. It was the same with fall or charity dinners—a person might be first served or last, depending on their karma. I thought it rigged, organizers spying which table housed their most friends and starting there.

Aha. Boyd Millhouse was standing near the bar with a few of his cronies. I slipped discreetly by and into the kitchen. Sure enough, there was Emma helping the catering staff finish final details for the midnight supper.

She caught sight of me and hurried over, her face aglow with excitement. "Is it time?"

I nodded. "Let's go."

We took the side door of the kitchen to keep us out of view of the front entrance. Hurrying down the street, we took a few short cuts and were soon in the alley behind the Millhouses.

"You keep a close watch, blow on this whistle"—I handed her a wooden train whistle that I had snafued from our childhood toy box—"and I'll slip right out."

"I'll watch from over there." She pointed at a tree near the fence. "That way I can keep an eye on the front and back entrances."

"Great. Wish me luck."

I headed around to the front door and rang the doorbell. No answer after a few more tries and I twisted the doorknob, expecting it to turn in my hands. It did not. *Hmm.* Maybe the back door after all? I scurried around to the back door, took a deep breath. *Please, please be unlocked.*

It was. I gave Emma a thumbs up and slipped inside the darkened home, grateful that I hadn't had to exactly break in. I mean, the door was unlocked, but my conscious still bit back.

I made my way to the living room and stopped in front of the seascape. *Perfect.* After removing the painting from the wall, I inspected the safe behind it. Just a wall mounted, inset type with a simple locking mechanism. *Easy-peasy.* I laid my hand over the keypad combination area and the numbers jumped into the visual section of my brain.

Two seconds later, I opened the small door and peered into the dark space at the few documents housed inside. I drew them out and discovered the map was the one on top. The other papers concerned a will and house ownership, not pertinent to the investigation, so I laid them back inside the safe, then took the treasure map over to a plugged-in night light to see better.

The thick paper, folded in four with deep creases, had yellowed with age and, turning it over, I discovered it had been drawn on the back of a gold claim document issued by the Province of Manitoba. It had been numbered and dated on the fourth day of July, nineteen ninety-seven. It was a legal and recognized claim…held in the names of three people. Terrance John Rail, Floyd Bernard Millhouse and Tegan Jane McCall.

What? The smoking gun implicated my auntie too? Stunned and confused, I held the incriminating document in one limp hand, unable to decide what to do next.

The piercing sounds of a train whistle decided it. I refolded, then hastily shoved the paper into the neckline of my dress. Slamming the safe shut, I hightailed it right out of there, my feet at least knowing what needed doing until my mind caught up with the stunning new facts. Until now, I would have sworn on a stack of grimoires that my auntie had nothing to do with the case except be in the wrong place at the wrong time. It looked like I was the wrong-headed one.

At the back door, I peered out into the yard through the built-in window. *No one in sight.* I opened the door and made a run for it, then nearly plowed Emma down when she dashed out from behind a telephone pole.

"Oh, thank goodness!" she said, her hand over her heart. "Sorry, that was a false alarm. The neighbor's dog banged into me as I was playing around with the whistle and I nearly swallowed the darn thing."

"That would be quite the feat since it's kind of huge." Like eight inches long and three inches in diameter.

She grinned. "So, did you get it? The treasure map?"

"Not only did I get it, but I also got serious proof of a connection between one of the dead guys and a couple of the suspects. "And if the DNA on the bones was conclusive, I was pretty certain we'd have evidence of a clear pattern. "Problem is, it implicates someone I was certain was totally innocent."

"Oh-oh. That's not good. Who is it?"

"I must swear you to secrecy. I need to get to the bottom of it before word gets out."

"Of course. You have my solemn word."

"Auntie T.J. is named along with Terrance Rail and Floyd Millhouse on a gold claim document issued by the Province of Manitoba."

Her expression was as stunned as I'd felt when I saw my auntie's name where I never thought it would be listed in a million freakin' years.

"Oh dear." Emma's face turned white and she began to chew on her bottom lip. "That doesn't look good."

"No wonder she's been ducking and diving the family for days. She's in this thing right up to her eyeballs. And to think Ace was giving her the benefit of the doubt." I shook my head in dismay.

"He's a keeper, that man."

"Yeah, well, when he finds out about this, I'm not certain he'll feel the same way about me." My heart rate accelerated and my stomach did a full somersault in sympathy.

"It's not your fault. This all happened *years* ago. He won't hold it against you."

"Maybe not, but my illegal attaining of the document, then hiding the facts from him of what it contains might be a game changer."

"Yeah, well, there is that." Emma grimaced in sympathy.

We had reached the hall again. I opened the side door and we slipped inside.

"I'm going to check on Ivana. Make sure she's happy."

"Cause *if Ivana's not happy, nobody's happy!*" Emma parroted the local folklore to try to coax a smile to my face. It barely worked. I was beyond upset about the situation. This had the potential for a fallout of major, gigantic, enormous proportions. I suddenly wanted to slip out of town myself.

"Ace has been looking all over for you," Tulip said by way of greeting, grabbing me by the arm and tugging me across the dance floor.

"Cheez, what is it with everyone hauling me all over the place tonight? First Ivana, then you," I grumbled.

"What's going on? Your body's so tense." She stopped mid-stride and looked me straight in the eyes.

"Nothing." I looked away. "Ah, there he is." I hurried over to Ace, who was standing near the bar and keeping a sharp eye on coming and goings. His presence would most definitely put the kibosh on overindulging.

He smiled at me, his expression alert. "I wondered where you had gotten off to."

"Just helping Emma with a girl thing."

He didn't ask more, thank goodness, but reached over and pulled a stray thread from the neckline of my dress. I swallowed, knowing what was on the other side. The incriminating document.

"I'm pleased to be invited tonight as your guest. I wanted you to know that."

Aww, talk about bad timing. Just when I had to hide something from him for the good of the family.

I licked my lips. "I'm happy you could come. You look really nice." He'd changed into a suit, something I had not seen him wear before, a charcoal number and a snowy white open-necked shirt that showed off his tan skin. *Delicious.*

"Would you like something to drink?"

"Just a soda, please." Though I wouldn't mind a bottle of Jack Daniel's or three, it would have to wait. I needed to be on my A-game.

I took a good look around the hall while Ace went to get my drink. Things appeared to be progressing smoothly, and since no one knew about Auntie's involvement, I still had time to solve this thing. I just hoped I could prove her innocent.

Hmm. There was time yet until the Promise Bags would be handed out. If I could slip away soon, I could go look for my auntie. *Track her down and tie her up.* I envisioned the scenario, getting the upper hand on the woman who was driving me to drink.

"You okay?" Ace asked, handing me a glass filled with soda. He looked suspicious now, like I had given something away. I looked down at my dress. No — the document was still hidden.

"Hand it over, darlin'."

"What are you talking about?"

"Whatever is hidden in your dress. I want to see it." He spoke the words close to my ear not to alert those milling around us.

"You said you couldn't read my mind!" Horror at what he had gleamed from my thoughts filled me with a sense of being trapped. *And exposed.*

"Keep your voice down," he cautioned.

"You promised me!" I hissed in his ear. "That you couldn't hear my thoughts."

"I can't always. Just when you're more emotional, I seem to be able to hear them. Stay calm, do the right thing and I won't be notified."

"That's impossible." I fumed, wishing the dance floor would swallow me whole.

"I don't think we're designed to be able to hide the truth from each other, whether we like it or not. I think we've been chosen."

The concept of being chosen stopped me in my tracks. "Do you really think so? That we're *chosen*?"

"I do. More than you know."

My heart squeezed and filled with wonder. No one had ever suggested such a thing before. Not in all the myriad books I had read, not in the numerous conversations I had had with girlfriends over what their boyfriends said, not in one thought I'd ever had about how relationships between men and women worked. *Nothing* compared to this moment.

"I don't know what to say." My heart squeezed again. And to think I was hiding something so important from him. It was wrong, on every level.

"Just tell me the truth and we'll be good. That's all I ask of you, Miss McCall."

"Okay. But not here. I want to share it when we're alone."

"Fine. Let's head outside. We can talk there. Did you bring a coat?"

"Yes, it's in the cloakroom."

"I'll get it." Ace strode off to get my wrap.

I waited by the bar, my thoughts in an uproar. Much as I wanted to keep things between us on a proper course, I felt like I would be betraying my family. I shook my head. No. It was Auntie T.J. who'd done that all on her lonesome.

Chapter Twenty-Four

Ace came back with my coat and helped me slip my arms into it.

"Where are you two going?" Emma asked, hurrying over from across the hall.

"Charm and I need to talk," Ace said.

Emma looked at him, then at me. "Everything okay? You need me to do anything?"

"Keep an eye out for Auntie T.J. You can't miss her. She's wearing a long coat, rubber boots and sunglasses. Oh, and send an all-out alert to the Northern Lights Coven. If anyone sees her, tie her to a chair and await future instructions. I'll be back to speak with her directly."

Emma's red eyebrows rose nearly to her hairline, but she didn't question my words. "Will do."

Ace and I headed to the entrance and out onto the parking lot.

"Want to walk or sit in my vehicle?"

"I think better when I'm walking."

"Okay, let's go."

The air had cooled since Emma and I had made our wild dash for the Millhouses' residence, and I gratefully took Ace's warm hand when he offered it.

"Beautiful night for a stroll and confession," he said, his tone noncommittal. Ace never failed to surprise me. Why was he even mixed up with me? I hid things from him. *Important things.*

"I understand how committed you are to your family. It's one of the things I admire about you."

"Quit reading my mind!" There wasn't as much bark to my tone as earlier. Ace was the real deal and deserved an explanation.

"I don't mean to, darlin'. It just happens. I imagine like your gifts just appear as well."

"I need to teach you how to control it ASAP."

"Maybe I don't want to learn how to do that."

I gave him a quick look. He was teasing, his lips quirking up into a smile. "It's important to me. I want to think my thoughts are my own."

He let out a deep breath. "I understand. We'll work on it together, okay? You can teach me all about it. Starting tomorrow."

"Deal. Okay, I have to tell you something you might not like."

"I know. Spill."

And so, I did, not leaving one detail out. Ace was a fair man. He'd go to the ends of the earth to find proper justice. Auntie T.J. was in good hands.

He took the document from me. "This is helpful. I can't say I like how you got it as it does constitute illegal search and seizure, but it will push along the investigation."

"I hope it speeds it to right the heck up. I desperately need to prove Auntie's innocence." *That is, if she's innocent in all this.* I hated thinking that and tossed the thought away as fast as it came to mind. I caught some movement from the corner of my eye and squinted in the twilight. The streetlights were just coming on, throwing shadows over the town. Someone was following us.

"We should get back. I have to hand out the goodie bags." A chill ran down my back and I gave an involuntary shiver.

"You cold?" Ace put his arm around me and I moved in nice and close. We strolled back to the hall. A few people were huddled outside having a cigarette, as smoking wasn't allowed on the premises. We got a few cheerful greetings on the way by.

"Your sister's in fine voice tonight. She's going to do our town proud in Hollywood," Susie Diamond said, putting her cigarette out in the container of sand designated for the purpose.

"Thanks. I know she'll try. She's been wanting this since forever."

Ace held the door open for me and in we went. Star was still on stage, singing a country and western classic, *Crying*, a ballad originally song by Roy Orbison. It suited her amazing voice, demonstrating her ability to hit the high notes with ease. I shivered again from the over-the-top emotion of the heartrending song.

I stood in the hall at Ace's side and took a moment to just enjoy things. Big changes were coming, and I couldn't stop them, but right now, at this exact moment in time, everyone appeared happy or at least content to enjoy the evening.

Emma came over and stood next to us. "She sounds fabulous tonight."

"She does."

"I heard what you're going to do, you know, for your mother. Star told me." The words hit me in the solar plexus and I just nodded, not trusting myself to speak.

"Soon as she's done singing, I'm going to announce everyone can come and get their Promise Bags."

Emma raised her eyebrows. "That sounds good."

The last haunting words of the song died away and Star took her customary bow before gliding off the stage. Darn, but that girl was graceful.

"I'll be back in a second." I weaved my way through the dancers now clapping loudly for my sister's performance, and up the steps to the stage.

"Evening, everyone. Time for the next event of the evening. If you'll line up, it's first come, first served for the Promise Bags. Let the games begin! Oh, and best of luck to all of you. May you get your hearts' desires." I stepped down onto the dance floor and joined Ace and the other couples for the walk past the display.

I picked up the midnight blue velvet bag and handed it to the constable. "Here you go. This should be an easy one for you, handsome. You already have the item on hand."

His eyebrows quirked upward as he gingerly took my offering.

"Don't be afraid. It won't bite you!"

We moved off to the side and he was about to withdraw the item inside when a loud voice shouted out an unexpected response, taking everyone's attention.

"Have you lost your darn mind, Maggie May? What in tarnation is this? You want another baby with the children finally out of our hair and settled? Are you crazy? My goodness, I thought you wanted an RV to travel the country! I put a down payment on one and everything!" Christopher Hale's voice rang out loud and clear.

"What? An RCMP shield? Why do you want to go and get training to join the police service when you're happy at home? What about my dinner?" Mike Smith shouted. His wife Wendy grabbed his bag and peered inside.

Ace opened his and pulled out a shiny ring with a large fake zirconium diamond included. I froze. What had gone wrong? I had been so careful, so protective.

"Well, this is unexpected, darlin'. But it does make me very happy." He grinned at me and before I could say a word, he took my left hand in his and dropped to his knees right there in front of everyone. What? He was going to do this! And I knew the man knew that I knew all about the mix-up! My heart filled with intense emotion. *There are no coincidences, sweeting.* Granny's voice echoed in my head.

The crowd went silent as the tableau, the one they'd all hoped for unfolded. I stood frozen to the spot as Ace cleared his throat, a tenderness in his expression that took my breath away. "Charm McCall, will you do me the honor of becoming my wife? I know it hasn't been that long that we've known each other, but a man knows when a woman is right for him. You bring out the best in me and I can't imagine a life without you in it. I want to replace this ring with the real thing, soon as I can. So please, if you'll have me, I'm prepared to wait for you. Just say yes and I will do my darndest to make all your dreams and wishes come true."

The crowd waited for my answer, hanging on to every word that Ace had so eloquently spoken. I swallowed hard, my hand fluttering to my throat. This was so unexpected. I'd just wanted my RCMP shield back that he had confiscated during the last investigation and here he was asking me to marry him. But maybe this was better?

"Say yes, Charm!" A voice rang out.

"Don't make the man wait! His knees are about to give out!"

"You don't have to say yes now, but please, say you'll think about it?" Ace's voice shifted, lost the firm edge of confidence that I so admired about him. I loved this man, had fallen for him months ago. Surely I could step up and let him know that? And what better way was there then saying I wanted to spend my life with him? If the goddess didn't approve, why had she brought him into my life? Ace had made my life better. And I had never met a more intriguing man. We just clicked on every level. Could I live without him? No. I truly didn't want to. And I didn't want him to regret his actions tonight. He might be pushing things, but I would have said yes in a few months anyway, so why not now?

I took a deep breath. "Yes, I'll marry you, Constable Ace Collins."

And at my simple words, he placed the ring on my finger and got to his feet. We embraced and kissed and the crowd went wild.

"Congratulations!"

Emma was all smiles as she came over. "You guys are perfect for each other. But what's going on? No one seems to have the right Promise Bag."

I shouted to get the crowd's attention. "I'm sorry, everyone. But there seems to be a mix-up tonight. I apologize." I went to the table and peered under it. My suspicions were confirmed. There was Brodie Jones, grinning like a Cheshire cat under the table, hidden by the tablecloth. When he caught sight of me, he made a break for it, racing to get away.

"Brodie Jasper Jones!" His mother's voice rang out as she ran after her son. "Wait until I get my hands on you!"

Star and Tulip came up to us, looking stunned and yet excited. It was a big moment. It had been just the three of us for twenty-one years, through thick and thin. Huge changes were afoot, and I could see the slight concern over what it would all mean in their clear blue eyes, though they were trying to hide it.

"I'm happy for you, sis," Tulip said, moving in to give me a hug. Star hugged me next and we all stood with megawatt smiles on our faces while the crowd worked to exchange the bags for their proper ones.

"That Brodie kid sure changed things tonight. First time anything like that's ever happened," Star said. She still looked a bit shell-shocked. Tonight, yes, it had been life-changing. But the more I thought about it, the happier and more excited I became. This was meant to be, otherwise, the bags would not have gotten messed with in the way they had. Bodie had just been the hand of fate. It was meant to be. Ace and I were perfect for each other. We loved and respected each other...and were willing to learn the rest.

Chapter Twenty-Five

Two hours later, I let myself in the back door of the Tea & Tarot. I was still jacked up on life, and adrenaline was still coursing through my veins. I'd kissed Ace goodbye at the door, wanting some alone time to absorb all the changes tonight had wrought.

"Well, baby Ling Ling, the times they are a-changin'." I threw my keys on the counter, slipped out of my coat and went to the cupboard to find a can of cat food.

"*Meow.*"

"Yeah, sorry, I'll make you some fresh perch in the morning. Right now, chicken will have to do, baby."

"*Meow.*"

"Glad you agree."

I placed the offering on a saucer and set it down for her. Throwing the tin in the garbage, I noted it needed emptying. I gathered it up, knotted the top and hurried to the back door to deposit the bag in the outside bin.

"Tell me where that map is right now! Or so help me, I'll squeeze the information out of you, Mountie or no Mountie." The voice hissed at me out of the darkness and a man dressed all in black with a matching ski mask confronted me. He stepped between me and the open doorway, effectively blocking me from getting back inside.

"How do you know I have it? Could have been anyone who took it."

"You were caught on camera stealing it earlier tonight. What would your precious Mountie think of that? His fiancé acting like a common thief."

"Boyd Millhouse." I was fairly certain that was the man confronting me, and I thought being offensive might make him take a step back, realizing he was exposing himself. "What did you do? Did you have something to do with the deaths of those men?"

"I already have one ghost haunting me—not like I couldn't handle another, sweetheart."

His cold, matter-of-fact tone chilled me to the marrow. So, the double aura Tulip had seen on the man meant he had a ghost-in-residence.

"Are you saying that you killed before? Were you responsible for the skeleton in the cave?"

"Wouldn't you like to know? You've got your nose in business that it don't belong in, sweetheart. I'm just here to give you clear warning. I want that map back tonight or I won't be responsible for what happens. Now hand it over."

"I don't have it. I gave it to the police. They now know that your name is on a gold claim, and that the other guy is long gone. I'm betting the bones are his, and that you had something to do with it."

"You're bluffing. I know you. You'll do *anything* to protect your family, even give up a kidney. Your aunt's name is on the document as well—we'll see who they come after. By the time this is figured out, I'll be long gone. Now, hand it over, or so help me I'll throttle it out of you."

"Okay. You're right about my not wanting my auntie's involvement revealed. But a little quid pro quo. Why did you do it, Boyd?"

He didn't correct me. "Why? The gold. It's always the gold. Terrance was looking to disappear with it, so I just took what was rightfully mine."

"But why kill again? Was that to cover up the first crime?"

"When his son came to town snooping around and making accusations, I knew I had to act and act fast. I've built a good life here that I couldn't let him take away from me. The poisoned moonshine was a nice touch."

"But if you're leaving anyway, why do it again?"

"Once you've crossed the line, it's easier the next time. Maybe my ghosts will make friends and leave me the heck alone now."

"You know that sounds crazy, right?"

"I'd hate to send you to the great hereafter, but don't push me. I'm reaching the end of my patience."

"Okay, okay. I'll give you the darned map. But you gotta know that if you harm me in any way that the full force of the RCMP will be brought to bear on you. Ace will see to that."

He grunted. "Not going to hurt you if you just hand the map over. You have my word on it. Now, let's go."

I backed inside the doorway, half stumbling against the door fame, trying to keep him in my line of sight. I didn't want to be attacked from behind. "It's over here somewhere. Was it you here the other day? Messing up my kitchen?" I went to the spot I had left the drawing of the map I'd drawn from memory, hoping I might fool him for just a second and gain the advantage.

"No, probably Buddy. He was sure when you wouldn't tell June where it was, that you were hiding something important. You're known for always finding stuff. You can blame yourself for that one."

"Did my auntie have anything to do with it?" I asked, rummaging through the sheets of paper, eyeing the nearby carving knifes set in the block of specialty wood.

"Nah, just her bad luck to be listed on the claim. All my doing." His hubris shook me to the core. The guy had the evil soul of a murderer. How had I not seen it before? His lust had protected him in a way, acting as a smokescreen to his true nature.

I handed him the paper. He took it eagerly, all his attention directed on the document. I grabbed the largest knife out of the set, my heart racing so loudly it throbbed painfully inside my skull. If I'd never had a migraine, I was fairly certain to get one after this experience. That was if I lived to have one.

"Say, this isn't the original document." He looked up to see me brandishing the wickedly sharp knife, the freshly sharpened edge gleaming in the overhead lights. "You cheated me!" He moved forward a step and I checked him with the outstretched blade.

"Stay back. I'm calling the police."

"What's going on?" came Ivana's voice. I had never been more grateful to hear her. She came up right beside me, stark naked, which explained my not hearing her approach. She had told me she always slept in the nude, and now I had proof. *More than enough proof.*

"You leave Charm alone, or I'll take you out, buster!"

The two of us confronted him. I wasn't certain which of us he was more scared of, the naked wild woman or me, but it worked. He backed down but seeming unable to stop himself from blessing me with one final warning. "You'd better watch your step."

Then he was gone.

"Oh my goddess." My legs turned to jelly and I slumped down on a stool. "That was too close."

"I'll call nine-one-one." Ivana picked up the phone and perfectly articulated our needs to the night person manning the detachment's phone. *Ah-ha.*

"Maybe you should put a robe on?" I suggested when she hung up the phone.

"Naked fine. Bother best friend?"

"A little. But thanks for being here. You saved my life." I would ignore her return to less-than-perfect English. I owed her a favor after all. Well, two now.

"Maybe. Okay, be back."

She left to head up the staircase as I tried not to look at her Aphrodite form, and in the quiet of the kitchen, my heart rate descended from the upper stratosphere and began to pump somewhat closer to normal earth speed.

"Charm!" Ace raced in the back door, his expression horrified. "Thank goodness you're all right!" We hugged long and hard, only breaking apart so I could share my story.

"Boyd will be arrested tonight. Are you all right if I leave now?"

"I'm good. Go do what you need to."

The back door opened and a gang of women came in. See? "I have my family now. I'll be okay."

Amid the chorus of concerned cries after Ace took his leave, I fell into form, letting everyone know I'd never been better. The culprit would be caught, my auntie was free to come home if she wanted once she got over herself and everything was going to be all right. My best guess on her situation was she'd been out at Skull Cave on a romantic tryst with Tweedy Bird and didn't want her sister to know. Then, when she realized the extent of the investigation, and with her name on the claim, she was hiding out until it was solved. She obviously knew she wasn't guilty.

"But you could have been hurt, sis. What were you thinking?" Star appeared most offended by my actions.

"Thinking I wanted to keep things on the up-and-up. You know I can't abide our town being upset. The sooner it was solved, the sooner we could all return to normal."

"Are you really okay, sweeting?" Granny Toogood asked, threading her fingers through mine, her soft voice holding all her caring for me. I looked down at the careworn hands of the woman who had worked a lifetime to keep bread on our table and clothes on our backs. She had surprised me, showing up so late when she should have been in bed. She'd congratulated me with the bestowing of a kiss on each cheek, saying she was pleased for me on my engagement, that I could not have set my cap for a finer man.

"I think so. And we can figure it all out from here, right?"

"Yes, I believe we can. You're made of stern stuff, sweeting. You'll go the distance, you and Ace."

"Thanks. He is one fine man." I closed my eyes for a moment, imagining how our life together might unfold. *You are chosen.* The words slipped through the cosmos and I listened, then humbly accepted.

Yes. That was true. Chosen to fill up all the parts of each other that would complete us, make us stronger as individuals, and as partners. Chosen to make a good life together, with family and friends. *Nothing finer than that.* Yes, I could forgive anything to have reached today, feeling the blessing of the universe. Hard knocks had made me who I was. And who I wanted to be going forward was a better person, more accepting of others, less judgmental and prepared to earn my own happy-ever-after...all with my handsome, caring Mountie by my side.

Thank you, goddess!

Want to see more from this author? Here's a taster for you to enjoy!

Sin City Wolf: Howl
January Bain

Excerpt

Cristaldo

I stared out at the night, the pull of the waxing moon yanking hard. Taking a gulp of my Dalmore 62, the finest single malt whisky ever produced, I raked a hand through my hair. The need to run free was building, growing stronger by the hour. I ached to let the clean, dry desert wind blow everything else away.

Blame it on the blood moon, an ominous portent to all my wild forbearers, scheduled to rise over Las Vegas's towering skyline in a matter of days. All my billions couldn't stop that trickster from wreaking havoc on my kind. Not that I would trade places with any otherworldly creature. *Nothing beats being a werewolf. Nothing.* Especially being a billionaire werewolf, with more money and possessions than any other wolf — and most humans — on the planet.

I savored the final gulp of the fragrant whisky with its drumroll and smooth finish. It would prove amusing to see what my rivals at the House of Ribelle had planned during the event, necessitating me showing those mongrels their low rank in the pecking order. My wolf bristled at the very idea, prepared to strike.

I dropped my glass onto the proofs of the recent interview I'd done for *Business Leader Quarterly*. The founding of the Royal Bank of Luceres and the recent expansion of our casino enterprises into several new countries was the stuff of legend and warranted a huge center spread in the magazine. Amusing really, humans being unable to see even that which what was right in front of their noses. My photo stared from the piece, all *GQ* to the public, but the slick surface hid a beast, one ready to burst forth at a moment's notice.

And that beast, bored and weary at the sameness of the days, needed a change. Where was the excitement? The new challenge? Having gathered all the riches the world had to offer didn't fill the deep void of longing, growing stronger by the day, of wanting something more. Only to myself would I admit that my life was lacking, that surrounded by so many, I was lonely.

Maybe it was time to choose a mate? Even if she wasn't the famed Forever Mate so valued by the pack, at least I would have company at night. Someone to share my victories with. *No.* I wanted the real thing. A true mate at my side, anointed as being the chosen one of destiny. I raised my head and closed my eyes, catching a sense of change on the wind. Something was coming…

Thud.

My office door slammed wide open, causing a low growl of warning to escape my throat before I caught sight of the intruder who'd broken my concentration. *Ah, Lucius. My identical twin.* He'd come bearing dubious gifts, by the look of it.

Two frightened young women preceded my brother inside the penthouse offices of the Glitter Palace casino.

They should be scared. Lucius might have been named for the light, but his heart was filled with darkness.

"I caught this pair skulking about, asking the dealers questions about our operation and generally making a nuisance of themselves. I intervened when they bribed one of our staff into letting them into the restricted area…bribed with the promise of a free blow job."

"That's not fair," the taller of the pair objected. They were beautiful women, tall and blonde and done up in the stock-in-trade of those looking for a good time. *Or to provide one.* I raised a sardonic eyebrow at her as she continued her protest.

"I'm just a student of hotel management, trying to get some pointers from those working in the real world. My friend Brandi only came along for company. I'm Jill, by the way."

Even from twenty feet away I could smell the smoking lie that scented her skin. Normally I would tell them both to strip, to prove themselves innocent. Today, I found the idea abhorrent. Lucius gave me a strange look, waiting for my reaction. I nodded at him. *You want this, go ahead.*

"Strip."

They both stared at Lucius with huge doe-like eyes.

"What?" Jill asked, her gaze flitting back and forth between me and Lucius.

"You heard me. If you're innocent, strip," Lucius said.

"I'm not wearing a wire."

"Prove it. I'll let you leave if you're clean."

The one called Brandi shook her head. "I'm not doing this. You can't make me." She hugged both arms around her upper body.

"I can and I will. We're the only authority here at the Glit." Lucius used the shortened version of the Glitter

Palace, our casino's name. His demands had aroused the taller one — her scent saturated the air with a sweet musk. My nose twitched, ambivalent about the odor.

"What's it to be, Jill? Strip or banishment?"

"So ban me. I don't care," Brandi said.

Jill looked my twin straight in the eyes, challenging him. She raised her arms in a graceful arc and undid the strings tied at the back of her neck, letting her short blue chiffon gown fall in a shimmer of fabric the length of her body to puddle on the floor. Underneath, she was naked except for a tiny pair of white lace panties. Her luscious double Ds were firm and upraised, the nipples tight and protruding out a good half inch, begging to be pinched and sucked. Apparently, Jill liked to be told what to do, like a long string of Jills before her. Bored now, my mind drifted. Even my wolf seemed to find the display less interesting than usual, just sitting back observing instead of wanting to play.

"See, no wire," she said. She twirled in a full circle, her long blonde hair cascading around her, her breasts swaying with the graceful ballet-like movements of her body.

"How about under those panties?" Lucius asked, the challenge clear. One thing we did agree on — there was nothing on earth more beautiful than the female body. But today, I sat and contemplated having another strong drink, drumming my fingers on my desktop.

She hooked her fingers into the elastic waistband and eased the panties down her long tan legs, exposing her complete Brazilian wax job. Then, slipping the lace over her four-inch platform heels, she threw them at Lucius. He caught them and took a deep whiff of their fragrant dampness. "Nice. Now you." He pointed at the other girl.

She shook her head. "No way."

I suddenly realized I'd prefer to go for a run than be here. The pent-up lust from the pull of the coming wolf moon made my skin ripple with the urge. If this female was reluctant, then banning her from the premises would suffice. Neither I nor Lucius would force a woman. Why should we, when they all came of their own accord? Not that I wouldn't mind a good chase for a change — as long as I won. *And I always win.*

"Fine. But be advised, a photo will be taken and shared with the staff," Lucius said. He was dragging this out and I wanted it over and done with. I tried to catch his eye to let him know.

The female hesitated, biting her bottom lip. I could see through the sham. I had to give it to them — the Ribelle dogs were attracting better-looking spies. Not brighter, perhaps, unless they were looking to be caught? They'd have to be checked over thoroughly before they could leave the premises. I'd leave those honors to my twin.

Lucius glanced my way, lust darkening his complexion. He, perhaps more than I, enjoyed our couplings with willing women in the immediate vicinity of the other. Our more studious younger twin brothers, currently in Rome, enjoyed having the *same* woman, but I did not imagine that ever being the case for me and Lucius, with me being alpha.

Spy number two shimmied out of her tight minidress, exposing another spectacular set of large breasts and a lack of underwear, her reluctance an obvious game. *And a lure.*

"I'll need to check you for bugs," Lucius said.

Jill, spy number one, offered herself to my brother, raising her hands high above her head in the surrender position. He caged her wrists between one of his hands, then ran his other hand through her hair, then down her supple flesh, tweaking her nipples before slipping his fingers down to her pussy. She arched her back.

From the corner of my eye, I caught the slight shimmer of the cosmic disturbance in the air around Lucius, his eyes flashing blue before returning to brown. He wanted the change. I got it. Business had been all-consuming of late, especially concluding the arrangements on the acquisition of the new bank.

A loud knock sounded at the door. "Come in," I called.

"Sorry to bother you, sire," Serge said with all due respect.

My right-hand man, second in line after Lucius and similar to a mafia don's *consigliere*, looked unusually agitated, though he was doing an admirable job of attempting to hide it. But *my* job was to miss nothing that might affect those I was in charge of. Every little nuance meant something.

"Yes?"

"Just advising you that the all-girl band, The Sirens, has arrived and is set up in Nero's." Serge was fully aware of my standing order to make sure I knew *everything* going on in my casino. The online contest we'd run for the chance to win three nights' playing at Nero's had drawn a lot of media attention — good for business, and good for the group that would benefit from the exposure.

I nodded. The sense of change in the wind tonight grew stronger. *Time to pay close attention*, it seemed to say.

The lights in the room dimmed. My twin was making preparations to fuck the women.

"Check their jewelry, Lucius. Remember the last time." Hiding a bug in an earring had worked until I'd had the penthouse swept for electronic devices.

I made a quick decision in the moment, born of my urge to get out of the office and check on the band that had drawn so much attention.

"Let's go," I said to Serge.

I led the way to my private elevator across the hall and punched the lobby number. We rode in silence, my wolf somewhat annoyed about losing out on the easy tail waiting upstairs in my office, now that I had chosen to move on. But my mind went back to thoughts of my own Forever Mate and what that would mean in my life.

I shook my head with finality, pushing the idea away. The chances of that happening after all this time were slim to none. But that didn't mean I couldn't enjoy the company of a female, under the right circumstances, to keep the urges at bay.

Moon madness is a bitch.

Home of Erotic Romance

Sign up for our newsletter and find out about all our romance book releases, eBook sales and promotions, sneak peeks and FREE romance books!

About the Author

January Bain has wished on every falling star, every blown-out birthday candle and every coin thrown in a fountain to be a storyteller. To share the tales of high adventure, mysteries, and full-blown thrillers she has dreamed of all her life. The story you now have in your hands is the compilation of a lot of things manifesting itself for this special series. Hundreds of hours spent researching the unusual and the mundane have come together to create a series that features strong women who don't take life too seriously, wild adventures full of twists and unforeseen turns, and hot complicated men who aren't afraid to take risks. She can only hope the stories of her beloved Brass Ringers will capture your imagination as much as they did hers when she wrote them.

If you are looking for January Bain, you can find her hard at work every morning without fail in her office with two furry babies trying to prove who does a better job of guarding the doorway. And, of course, she's married to the most romantic man! Who once famously replied to her inquiry about buying fresh flowers for their home every week, "Give me one good reason why not?" Leaving her speechless and knocking her head against the proverbial wall for being so darn foolish. She loves flowers.

January loves to hear from readers. You can find her contact information, website details and author profile page at https://www.totallybound.com

www.ingramcontent.com/pod-product-compliance
Lightning Source LLC
Chambersburg PA
CBHW031451260626
47154CB00016B/837